TAKEDOWN

Riley "Bear" Logan Book Three

L.T. RYAN

Liquid Mind Media, LLC

THE JACK NOBLE SERIES

Receive a free copy of The Recruit by visiting http://ltryan.com/newsletter.

CHAPTER ONE

Bear let the crowd push him out of Penn Station and dump him on the sidewalk. He immediately had to sidestep a man with a briefcase who was trying to get around an old woman without knocking her over. After a few attempts to get out of everyone's way, Bear backed up against a wall and took a second to breathe the city in.

Bear didn't make a habit of looking at Manhattan's buildings in wonder. That was saved for the tourists. New York City was a beautiful place if you liked steel and glass, but even natives got tired of the bustle after a while. The city had a way of sapping your energy, of making you see the worst of humanity.

He held back a laugh. Bear had seen plenty of the worst of humanity over the last several weeks, and New York felt shiny and new in comparison. He'd been away from home for too long, and he was ready to lay low for a while. Maybe pick up a couple jobs here and there doing something menial while he kept his ear to the ground. He knew some people who'd do him a favor, who'd be willing to look the other way for a short time.

And it would be a short time. Bear was not naïve enough to think all his troubles were over. Not while Jack was still missing, at least.

Bear sucked in another deep breath of city air, a confusing mixture of putrid garbage and mouthwatering food stands. His stomach growled, but he ignored it. There'd be time to eat later. For now, he had to go knock on a couple doors.

He hefted his backpack over his shoulder and started walking down 8th Ave. He didn't have much on him, but he had a place nearby with the basics. Unfortunately, he knew that if he went back there now, he'd sleep for three days. And as good as that sounded, he needed to get some things done first.

He didn't even make it to the corner before some guy in a suit knocked into him. Bear opened his mouth to say something when he felt a piece of paper being slipped into his hand. His first instinct was to reach out and grab the guy before he could take off, but it was already too late. The man had been a head or two shorter than him, disappearing easily into the crowd. Bear debated going after him, but by the time he caught up, the other guy would be waving to him from the other side of a subway car door. Not worth the effort.

He pressed himself against the façade of a building and let the stream of people adjust to passing around him. He watched them for a moment, looking left and right, looking across the street. No one paid him any attention. No one stuck out. Looked like the guy in the suit had been alone.

The paper had only two words written on it: *Bryant Park*.

Bear popped his neck and looked around him again. He didn't recognize the handwriting. Didn't know who could want a meeting with him so soon after landing. That meant they'd been watching him this whole time. There were too many options to choose from. Did it have anything to do with Korea? With Jack? With something else?

All of the unknown factors made the back of Bear's head itch, but he ignored it. Instead, he turned around and started heading back up 8th, toward Bryant Park. It was probably reckless, but he was getting tired of being tugged back and forth like someone's plaything. Maybe he could put an end to this now.

He sighed, some of his anger dissipating. He didn't blame Sadie for playing him like she did in Korea. He knew she meant well, and if he were honest with himself, he felt much better knowing Thorne wasn't in the wind anymore. Sadie's plan to bring Thorne out of hiding had been a solid one, even if it did end up getting them both in more trouble than they were comfortable with.

Then again, he'd pretty much been neck-deep in trouble since the day he met Jack Noble. And for some reason he wasn't exactly ready to change that just yet. Maybe he had a death wish. Maybe he just knew he'd never actually be satisfied working a boring job for the rest of his life.

But if someone wanted to meet him in Bryant Park, they weren't looking to blow his brains out. There'd be plenty of people there, plenty of witnesses. The park would be a mixture of traffic noises and the sound of people talking and laughing and going about their day. Perhaps a show going on in the center lawn. There were several exits, and a subway entrance Bear could slip into if he found himself needing an escape.

So why was the back of his head still itching?

Bear pushed his way toward 40th Street and crossed over, making his way toward 6th Ave. He kept his eyes sharp, but there were too many people to do a proper assessment. Whoever this was could have a dozen men or women on his tail, switching out every couple blocks, and Bear would be none the wiser. Or maybe he was utterly alone in the crowd. He wouldn't know until he met the person behind the note.

Bear jogged up the steps to Bryant Park and stuck to the outer rim. There was a huge inner field roped off with a sign that read *special event*, but he already felt exposed as it was. He wasn't about to make it easier for them.

Instead, Bear made a single loop around the park, scattering gravel and pretending to scroll through his phone while clocking as many people as he could out of the corner of his eye. He didn't recognize anyone, not from the walk over and not from the vast catalog of faces in his memory bank.

But whoever this was knew him. It wasn't hard to pick his thick six-six frame out of the crowd, and walking around in circles wasn't doing him any favors. So Bear found an empty chair right off the path and sat down. There was no way he could watch the street behind him and the entrances to his right and left at the same time. That was probably the point.

Instead, he settled in and did the best he could to look unimposing. That was never an easy task for him, but with his phone in his hand and his elbow perched on the bistro table, most people just figured he was another regular guy waiting to meet up with an old friend and trade stories.

Five minutes passed. Then ten. Then fifteen. His stomach knotted. His knee bounced. Whoever this was seemed to be as paranoid as him. That didn't bode well for either of them.

When a full twenty minutes had transpired, Bear stood up. He was tired of wasting his time, and maybe it would force them to show. Either way, he was done waiting. The itch had spread from the back of his head down to his shoulders. He needed a shower.

He made it three steps when a young woman's voice sounded behind him.

"I'm sorry I kept you waiting, Bear." She paused while he turned around. "I had to make sure you were alone."

Bear blinked several times. Out of everyone he could've expected, Thorne's little protégé Maria hadn't even cracked the top fifty.

CHAPTER TWO

The last time Bear had seen Maria, she'd been blonde. Now her hair was red and fell in soft curls around her shoulders. This was quite a difference from the dirty, beaten, drugged-up girl he'd rescued just a few weeks ago.

She'd also had a gun held to her head on his orders. He'd had no intention of killing her, not then, and not now, despite her ties to Thorne. The look of betrayal in her eyes when Thorne had said he was willing to sacrifice her made Bear think he could trust her.

Then again, she could also be a wild card. Her mentor threw her to the dogs and didn't even bother cleaning up the mess. And now he was behind bars. She was either back in the game or working on her own for motives only known to her. Neither would bode well for Bear.

"You're just about the last person I expected to see." Bear eased back down in his chair and motioned to the one next to him, keeping a guy in a suit in his periphery.

Maria did a quick scan of the area and then sat down, crossing her legs and facing him. She offered a meek smile. "I bet that doesn't happen often. Being surprised like that, I mean."

"It doesn't." Bear didn't give up any other information. She wanted to meet *him*, after all.

"No hard feelings about last time we saw each other." She tossed her hair over her shoulder. "I'm glad Thorne got what he deserved."

"You and me both."

"You're probably wondering why I asked you here."

"I am."

Maria looked around once more and scooted her chair a little closer. "I need help, Bear. And you're one of the few people I trust these days."

"Me? What kind of help?" He couldn't stop himself from scanning the area around them as well. He'd assumed he was being watched by whoever had asked him to come to Bryant Park, but what if *they* were being watched as well? That was trouble he didn't need.

"I'm trying to wrap up loose ends. With Thorne out of the picture, I'm not really sure what's left for me."

Bear crossed his arms and stayed silent.

Maria continued. "Sadie's been helping the best she can. The CIA can't exactly take me in as one of their own, but they've been treating me like a trusted asset. They want to know everything they can about Thorne. I told them as much as I could, but he wasn't exactly the sharing type. And the drugs I was forced to take, the effect they had on me, I'm still not back to being clearheaded."

Again, Bear decided silence was his best course of action.

"I tried putting out feelers, to find anyone who may have talked to Thorne. That's when I came across something strange." Maria took a deep breath before continuing. "Three agents have gone missing in London. I was their liaison while I was working for Thorne. It was pretty easy work. Good practice. Slipping in and out of crowds, passing along information. No one suspected me. I could disappear easier than someone like—"

"Me?"

Maria cracked a smile, but it looked sad. "Yeah, someone like you."

"Why'd they go missing?"

She shrugged. "Don't know. I thought I passed credible intel on to them. I'm beginning to think that was a setup, too." Maria looked directly at Bear now, her eyes glistening. "I don't know what to believe anymore, Bear. This whole life was fine when I thought I was on the right side of things, but now that I know what Thorne was mixed up in, I'm second-guessing everything."

"What does this have to do with me?" he asked.

Maria tilted her head back and stared up at the sky for a few seconds. Bear could see when her face hardened into a mask of determination. She looked back at him and her eyes were dry again. "I need your help."

"Yeah. Why *me*? Why not go to Sadie?"

"I don't know who to trust," Maria said. "Thorne told me horror stories about the CIA. I trust Sadie, I do, but she runs things by the book. She might want to do the right thing, but not everyone she works with feels the same way. Believe it or not, you're pretty transparent, Bear. I can trust you'll make the right call."

Bear laughed and ran a hand over his head. "Look, kid, I just got home. I've got enough on my plate. I have a bad habit of taking on other people's problems. I'm starting to think I need to break that habit."

Maria looked torn between frustration and desperation. "I thought you were supposed to be one of the good guys."

"You don't know me."

Now Maria looked angry. "Out of the two of us, I know I owe you a hell of a lot more than you owe me. It wasn't easy coming to you. I know what you've just been through. I know you probably just want some peace and quiet. But I—"

Maria's words choked off as her voice broke. She cleared her throat and took a second to regain her composure. "I've killed a lot of people for Thorne. Or at least been responsible for their deaths. There's more than that. I was following orders, but, that's just an excuse. I know I'm not a good person. I'm selfish. For so long, all I cared about was surviving. Then Thorne showed me how strong I could be. How much good I could do. I started to care. It'll probably be my downfall."

Bear chuckled. "You and me both, kid."

"These were good agents, good people. One of them had just gotten married. Had a kid on the way. He was only a few years older than me. If I did something wrong here, I owe it to them to fix it. I owe it to myself. Because if I don't, I'm afraid that's gonna be it for me. Then I won't be any better than Thorne."

Bear ran his hand through his beard. Maybe he would've said yes on a different day. But he was exhausted to his core. His feet had barely hit the ground before something else had fallen into his lap. He needed to stay focused. He needed to find Jack.

"I'm sorry." Bear stood up. "I want to help you, I do, but I have my own shit going on. I need to take care of some things first. I don't know how long it'll take. Maybe after that. I don't know."

Maria stood up with him. "Bear, please. Even if you just ask around. Anything will help. I don't know who else to go to."

Bear opened his mouth to tell her he'd consider it after his business was done, but four figures closing in around them made him stop short.

CHAPTER THREE

The four men came at them in pairs from either side of the path. The only exits were through the hedges or through the lawn. Neither way could outrun a 9mm. The men separated to form a wall around Bear and Maria. They were wearing street clothes, but Bear knew they were agents the second he spotted them. To anyone else it would just look like a group of friends standing around having a chat. That meant they wanted to keep things quiet. It was the only good thing about this situation.

Bear kept his stance neutral. "Can I help you, boys?"

The guy with a bruised eye spoke first. He was beefier than the others, like he'd been a linebacker his whole life until Langley showed up at his door with an incredible offer. "I believe you can, Mr. Logan. Will you please follow us?"

He and the man to his left parted and motioned for them to walk. Bear didn't budge.

"Who's asking?"

"A friend," the linebacker said. "Look, we don't want any trouble. You could walk away now, but my boss will just keep asking. Maybe you can save us all a little time?"

Bear's hackles were still raised, but there was less alarm to it now. He was used to subtle threats. This was more like a cordial invite. Still, it was better to play along. If he got a chance to slip away, he'd take it.

Maria looked up at Bear and he met her eyes. "Go home, kid. I'll be in touch."

"Her too," the linebacker said. "My employer would like to speak with you both, please."

Bear looked at the four men in front of him. They all looked tuned into their surroundings but stood calm. Bear wasn't looking for a fight. Neither were they. He just hoped Maria wasn't going to end up in the middle of something she was going to regret.

Bear looked over at the linebacker. "Where?"

"There's a nice café just down at the corner. Pretty popular place. You should find something you like there."

Bear nodded and the linebacker and his partner led the way out of Bryant Park. The other two men kept their distance, but Bear felt them at his back like they were practically walking on his heels. Bear let a few people pass in front of him, but he didn't bother trying to break off. He couldn't leave Maria, and he wasn't sure if she'd follow him if he took off running.

Better to just see this through.

The linebacker led the group across the street and to the corner café. He and his partner kept walking for a few paces, then stopped to lean against the wall, watching as people came and went, none the wiser.

Bear got the hint. He opened the door to the café and motioned for Maria to walk through first. If something was going to happen to them, it would be outside the coffee shop. He paused in the doorway and looked back for the other two men who had been trailing them, but they'd disappeared. He had a feeling they weren't far.

The café was tight and full of people. The chatter was loud and competed with the clinking of spoons inside thick ceramic mugs. It smelled like fresh brew and bread. Bear inhaled it. He could use something to eat. Probably some coffee, too.

But his thoughts were cut short when Maria groaned. Bear looked down at her, then followed her gaze to a table in the back. There was no mistaking Sadie's coy smile. Bear stifled a groan of his own.

A heavyset woman with messy hair and what Bear supposed was a permanent scowl stopped in front of him. "Two?"

He blinked at the question. "I'm sorry?"

Her scowl deepened. "Table for two?"

"No." Bear pointed at the table in the back. "Meeting a friend."

The woman looked over her shoulder. "Coffee?"

"Yes, ma'am."

"Two," Maria added, then started moving toward Sadie. Bear followed. Under her breath, she asked, "Friend?"

"More or less." He didn't hold anything against Sadie for putting him in the middle of the Thorne business. Figured he would've found himself there one way or another, regardless.

"She's a pain in the ass," Maria muttered.

"Didn't you just say you trusted her?"

Maria held up her index finger like she was giving a lecture. "Just because you trust someone doesn't mean they're not a pain in the ass."

He grinned as he thought of Jack. "True."

Bear reached the table first and smiled down at Sadie. "Wasn't expecting to see you again so soon."

Sadie forced a laugh, sending ripples through the coffee in the mug held in her hand. "Me neither. Was kind of hoping I could leave you alone for a while." Her smile faded. "I'm sorry about the escort."

"Were all four guys necessary?" Bear asked. "And all this business about *my employer*?"

"Can't be too careful these days," Sadie said.

Bear shrugged. "I get it."

"Appreciate that." Sadie paused while the scowling waitress

brought him and Maria a pair of coffee cups and filled them to the brim. Once she left without asking if they needed anything else, Sadie continued. "Why'd you take the long way home, Bear?"

"Can't a guy take a vacation?"

"We both know that's not what you were doing."

He didn't deny it. After Sadie had let Bear out of her sights, he could've gone straight home. Instead, he flew to London and started putting out feelers. Thorne asking if he'd talked to Jack lately made Bear want to go on the offensive. Jack had disappeared before, but nothing like this.

No one knew where he was.

No. One.

Jack and Bear had known each other for long enough that they had several contingency plans in place. Bear didn't know all of Jack's hideouts, but he knew most of them. He knew who Jack would go to if he needed help. He knew where he would leave him messages if he could.

But there was nothing to find. It was like Jack had just slipped out of existence.

That meant one of two things. Either Noble had needed to go deep underground, or someone else had gotten to him first. Neither situation sat well with Bear.

"I was looking for Jack," he said. There was no point in hiding the truth. Sadie already knew the answer. "No leads."

Sadie took a long sip of her coffee, but Bear still saw the way her lips turned downward. He didn't know what was going on between them, whether they were just friends or something more, but he knew they cared about each other. She'd help him if she could.

She set her cup on the table. "I haven't heard anything either. And that's not why I asked you here today."

"Why am I getting the feeling I'm not going to like what comes next?" Bear sat up, realizing he'd been conned. He looked over at Maria and waited for her to make eye contact. "Were you in on this?"

"Not intentionally," Sadie said as Maria's cheeks reddened. "We planted the idea in her head hoping she'd reach out to you."

Maria threw her hands out. "Because telling me to get in contact with Bear would've been too easy, right?"

"We have to be careful." Sadie kept her eyes on Bear. "I don't know what's going on here, Bear. That makes me uncomfortable."

"Well I'm here now." He leaned back and drained his mug. "Fill me in."

CHAPTER FOUR

B ear landed at Heathrow just after 7 a.m. local time. He stifled a
yawn, and stretched as soon as he was off the plane. He felt
hungover thanks to the pill cocktail he took to ease his anxiety prior to
taking off. It hadn't exactly been an easy rest, but he'd at least slept
for the majority of the eight hours it took to get to London. It didn't
hurt that Sadie had sprung for business class.

As he made his way to customs, he replayed their conversation in
his head. What she had told him lined up with what little information Maria had shared. A few agents had gone missing in the London
area, presumably because Maria had unintentionally given them bad
intel.

What made the whole situation more interesting, and the reason
why Bear had decided to hop on yet another plane, was that these
agents had been Sadie's operatives. They were in London to aid MI5
in terrorism control in the city and had appeared to have been used in
an unsanctioned operation. The whole deal had Thorne written all
over it, and while it wasn't much to go on, it was the only lead Bear
had on Jack's possible location.

But it was a thin thread. Thorne wasn't going to talk, they all knew that, and there was no evidence that what had gone down in London was in any way connected to Jack. Then again, it was clearly something Thorne was trying to do under the radar. Both Bear and Sadie figured if it didn't lead to Jack, it would at least help bury Thorne that much deeper.

So Bear slid through customs without a hitch thanks to the documents Sadie had provided him. He trusted she had his best interests in mind, and even if she didn't, he trusted she was a good agent. At least this time she had met him face-to-face prior to dragging him into another situation. He had to respect that.

She'd tried to apologize again, but he'd waved her off. Having Thorne locked up had made it all worth it, not to mention they now knew something was going on with Jack. Bear couldn't help wondering how long it would've taken him to realize Noble was missing if Thorne hadn't tipped them off.

His second biggest question—after where the hell was Jack?—was why Thorne had said anything at all. The guy clearly didn't have all his marbles, even if he was a brilliant spy. Bear couldn't believe Thorne had tipped them off to help, which meant it was a trap. Or, worse yet, it was playing right into a bigger scheme he couldn't even see yet.

Bear shook the feeling and walked up to the rental car counter and got the cheapest car he could find. Part of him wanted to check out the more expensive rides, but he knew if he saw them, he wouldn't be able to resist. Sadie was footing the bill for this little trip, after all. But he needed to blend in, and a well-used and moderately priced vehicle would do the trick. He'd tried to tell this to Noble time and again, but Jack enjoyed the Audi lineup way too much.

Car keys in hand, Bear walked out through the door and into the English air. It was nearing the end of April, which meant the weather could go either way. Today, it was a little cloudy, but relatively warm. It had just rained, and the moisture clung to his skin. Still, it felt refreshing compared to the stuffy seat he'd crossed the Atlantic in.

He didn't linger before getting his vehicle and heading away from the airport. He was only five minutes out when Sadie called. Right on time. So far they were off to a smooth start, but he knew better than to bank on this being an easy job.

He sat the phone on his lap and put it on speaker and answered.

Sadie's voice came through loud and clear. "How was the flight?"

"Pretty terrible from what I remember of it."

Sadie chuckled. "You need to get over the flying thing, Bear."

"Yeah, yeah. I'll get over it when I'm dead."

"Let's hope that's a long time from now." The sound of papers being shuffled in the background filled the silence. "Everything else going smoothly?"

"Yep. Just wanted to thank you for setting me up in this nice BMW. I'm not used to traveling in style."

"Hilarious. We both know you're not that stupid."

"Yeah, but sometimes I wish I was." Bear looked out over the hood of his little Hyundai and frowned. "They never seem to make cars big enough for me."

"One of these days, Bear. One of these days."

"But not today."

"Not today." Sadie paused. "I have a contact for you."

Bear straightened up as best he could in the tiny vehicle. "I'm all ears."

"He's a little flighty, so make sure you've got some cash on you."

"Are you sure he's even going to show then?"

"He'll be there. He's reliable. He just gets spooked easily."

"Great." Bear changed lanes and checked his mirrors. It seemed like an average day. For now. "It's not like people tend to get spooked around me, or anything."

"He knows to look for you. Not by name, just general description. He'll meet you at a restaurant. Just grab something at the bar and wait. He'll approach you."

"What kind of information does he have?"

"He said he could fill you in about the comings and goings of the agents before they disappeared."

Bear gripped the wheel tighter. "Any reason why he didn't just pass that information on to you?"

"Like I said, he's a little paranoid. He only works face-to-face, and I'm not going to be there for another day or so. I've got a lot of paperwork to deal with first."

"Maybe it's a trap."

Sadie didn't respond right away. "Possibly, but I doubt it. This guy's helped me out before. I trust him."

Bear checked his mirrors again before answering. He could already feel the paranoia settling in. "Thorne's smart..."

"We both know that. But this is the best I have for now, Bear. I'll keep digging." She shuffled some papers again. "I'll text you the address."

"Copy that."

Bear drew in a deep breath and slowly let it out. He liked being able to travel as much as he did—slip in and out of crowds unnoticed. He liked the freedom of working just outside the lines of society. It was exciting. Better yet, it was liberating.

But paranoia constantly threatened to steal those feelings away. He had been looking forward to not having to look over his shoulder for a couple of months. He was smart, he knew that, but Thorne had already proven he was typically one step ahead of them.

And Bear couldn't shake the feeling this was one of those times.

CHAPTER FIVE

Against his better judgment, Bear made his way into a restaurant named Cataldi's. Searing steak overwhelmed his senses. He fought against his knotting stomach to take in the rest of the place. It was all rough-sawn hardwood floors, seasoned by age and use. The lights were slightly dimmed, but still bright enough so aging eyes could read the menu without anyone complaining loudly for the other customers to hear. It felt like a family establishment, decorated haphazardly but with plenty of love.

Bear made his way over to the bar and sat down, cataloging everyone he passed along the way. The dinner rush had ended an hour or two ago. Now the restaurant was just full of stragglers and regulars. There was a family of four in the corner, a few older men at the bar, and one or two young couples sharing a drink along the opposite wall. No one looked like they were there for him.

Rustling behind the bar drew Bear's attention. He leaned forward and saw a woman rifling through boxes on one of the shelves. She had raven hair that fell to the middle of her back and a lean, athletic frame. She wasn't someone you'd want to piss off.

After a moment she stopped, put her hands on her knees, and stood up so quickly she almost knocked heads with Bear.

"Can I help you?" she asked, looking him up and down. Her eyes were bright with suspicion.

Something about the woman's frustration made Bear feel like he was looking in on something private. "Fullers?"

Her face remained immobile. "I don't work here."

Before Bear could ask her what she was doing behind the bar, a man stepped out of the back, wiping his hands on a rag.

"They're back here, Sasha."

Sasha cast another glance at Bear before walking into the back without another word.

"Be with you in a moment," the man said.

Bear nodded and watched as the two of them disappeared behind the doors. He noted the encounter with the woman, but didn't think much of it. He had more important things to worry about.

A minute or two later, the man from the back emerged and Bear asked for his beer again. Once it was placed in front of him, he took a long pull and swept his eyes around the restaurant for a second time. One or two people had swapped out with new customers, but Bear was sure none of them were his contact.

By the time Bear had finished his second beer, he had half a mind to call Sadie and tell her the contact was a no-show. But just as he put his hand in his jacket, someone bathed in cheap aftershave slid onto the stool next to him.

The man held up his hand for the barkeep. "Guinness, please."

Bear kept silent. He wasn't about to break the ice between them on the off chance this guy really just wanted a beer while sitting next to a large American man in a mostly empty bar. If the guy was as paranoid as Sadie said he was, Bear wasn't going to do anything to risk putting him on edge.

The man waited until he had his beer and the bartender returned to the back room. He didn't turn toward Bear when he asked, "Mr. Logan, I presume?"

His accent was rough, like a mix between the kind of English the Queen would scoff at and something from Eastern Europe. Without looking at him, Bear couldn't place his ethnicity. Given how paranoid this guy was supposed to be, maybe that was on purpose. Was the accent even real?

Bear tipped his head. "And what should I call you?"

"Mr. Jones is fine."

"You're late."

Mr. Jones took a swig of his beer. "Had to be careful. Didn't want any unexpected company."

"Are you expecting some?"

The man shrugged. "The second you're not expecting it—"

"It shows up," Bear finished.

Mr. Jones raised his glass. "You got cash for me?"

"You got information for me?"

Bear turned toward Mr. Jones for the first time and studied his face. He was older than Bear had expected. His face was dark and weathered, like he'd worked outside in the sun his whole life. Gray hair fell down to the tops of his ears, and a gray beard covered the majority of his face. Bear had a feeling that if he cut his hair and shaved the beard, he'd look like someone completely different. That was probably the point.

"Money first," Mr. Jones said. "Our mutual contact knows the deal. I figured she'd pass that information on to you."

"Our mutual contact is more trusting than I am."

Mr. Jones shrugged and drained the rest of his beer and slid one foot to the floor. "You need the information more than I need the money, friend. It's up to you."

Bear gritted his teeth and pulled an envelope from his jacket. He didn't miss the way Mr. Jones twitched. "I don't have time for your bullshit."

Mr. Jones at least had the decency not to look pleased when he won their little standoff. Instead he pocketed the cash and slid a piece of paper toward Bear. "That's the address where they had been coming and going for weeks."

Bear peeked at it to make sure it wasn't blank, and then pocketed it. He didn't recognize the area.

"Their routine was pretty regular. Too regular, if you ask me."

"What do you mean?"

"Routine breeds complacency. If anyone wanted to go after them, they'd be easy to find." Mr. Jones took another sip of his Guinness before he continued. "Out by nine, back by lunch, out again an hour later. They'd return home around dinnertime, or on occasion, they'd come back by midnight. Never later. They ordered a lot of Indian food. And then it all just stopped."

"When was this?"

"A couple weeks ago. Honestly, I expected someone to come looking for them right away. But no one did. I figured they had moved on until our mutual contact came asking about them."

"Why were you watching them to begin with?" Bear asked.

Mr. Jones smiled. "I don't think you need that information, Mr. Logan."

Bear could tell he was gonna hit a brick wall with this guy. He finished the rest of his drink and threw a couple bills down on the bar. "How do I find you again?"

Mr. Jones' eyebrows knitted together, but he never lost the sparkle in his eye. "Why would you need to find me again?"

"In case things go sideways." Bear paused. "Or in case you lied to me."

"Then you have nothing to worry about, Mr. Logan." He reached over and brushed something off Bear's shoulder. "My job was to provide you with the address of the building they had occupied and to tell you about their routine. Anything after that is on you."

Bear didn't know what it was about this guy that set him off. He was used to dealing with flighty people, but Mr. Jones was different. He relished it. It was like a game to him. And with Jack's life on the line, Bear didn't have the patience for that kind of attitude.

But if he needed to talk to Mr. Jones again, it sounded like Sadie knew how to get in contact with him. So instead of answering, Bear stood up and walked away.

It was time to get some rest and then do some digging on his own.

CHAPTER SIX

When Bear woke up the next morning, it took him a minute to place where he was and what he was doing there. He'd grabbed a hotel on the outskirts of London late at night and checked in with Sadie to give her an update. The conversation was brief, which didn't bother Bear. He still felt off following the cocktail he'd taken to get on the plane. He'd needed to sleep.

He sat up and stretched. His head felt clearer, but that only made matters worse. His meeting with Mr. Jones the night before still wasn't sitting well with him. The guy was paranoid, sure, but he went through a lot of trouble just to slip Bear an address. The price tag on that information seemed a little steep.

He'd decided as he was falling asleep that it was time to hit up his own contacts. He knew a couple people in London who'd be willing to help him out, especially if he mentioned that Jack was in trouble. The two of them had built up quite a network over the years, and Bear was thankful for that now more than ever.

The shower was hot and did wonders to finish waking up Bear's body. He did his best to tame his beard, but as usual it was a losing battle. Anyone who knew him would be surprised he wasn't covered in cuts and bruises. By all standards, he was looking pretty good this morning.

Probably wouldn't last.

Bear wondered, not for the first time, how Jack was faring. If he was deep in hiding, then there was nothing to worry about. He was probably eating beans out of a can and enjoying a good book. Bear imagined him in the middle of the woods, living off the land. Maybe he even had a dog.

Worst case scenario? Jack was dead. Bear didn't like to linger on that thought. Jack was tough. He'd gotten out of situations with impossible odds before. No way Noble was going to let Thorne get the best of him.

But that didn't mean Jack was in good shape. Maybe he was just in hiding. Or maybe he was being tortured. Jack could take a lot before he cracked. Still, Bear didn't want to waste any time. If anything, Jack would give him shit for dragging his feet as much as he had already. He wasn't looking forward to that earful.

There was still no evidence that the missing agents had anything to do with Jack's disappearance, and Bear was itching to get some answers on that front. If someone wanted to wipe the evidence from the building the agents were staying in, it'd be gone already. If there was anything left to be found there, it'd keep for a day or two.

Bear made a mental search for people he could trust in London and cross-referenced that with those who might have heard anything about Jack. A couple names stood out, but one in particular seemed like the smart choice: Dottie.

Tracking her down was easier than it should've been considering Dottie had been an agent for MI5, but she knew how to disappear when she needed to. Since that wasn't the case here, Bear figured it was a good sign. No one was looking for her as far as he knew, which meant a meeting with him would go relatively unnoticed.

Or at least he hoped. That tingle of paranoia was still sitting firmly in the back of his head.

But Dottie knew how to pick a good location too. They met at a busy restaurant, something a bit more commercial than the place where he'd met Mr. Jones, but it served their purpose. Big crowd. Lots of noise. No one would be listening in, and the overworked wait-staff wouldn't be checking in on them every two minutes.

Bear arrived first and walked around the block twice to make sure he wasn't being followed. No one stood out, so he entered the restau-rant and got seated after a few minutes. The place was packed wall-to-wall with tables and chairs. He had requested a spot in the back corner, and even though he had to squeeze in against the wall, it would be worth it for the additional privacy.

Dottie walked in ten minutes later. Bear had already ordered a cup of coffee and was halfway through it when he spotted her. He attempted to get up out of his seat, but she held up her hand to stop him.

"I'm not sure you'd be able to get back in there again, Mr. Logan. Better not chance it."

Dottie's accent was clean and posh. It was either the result of fancy schooling or a lifetime of making sure she sounded like a proper English lady. Bear wouldn't be surprised if it was the latter. A neutral accent didn't stand out as much.

Bear always forgot Dottie was a bit older than him and Jack, and it took a minute to realize it. Her skin was smooth and her hair was either dyed to look natural or she was lucky enough to be one of those women who never had to worry about grays. She might not have been as lean and toned as she used to be, but Bear had no doubts she could handle herself. She'd been in this game longer than he had, and he didn't want to test her limits.

Luckily, there was little chance this meeting would come down to that.

"Thanks." Bear shifted in his seat, trying to find a more comfort-able angle. "Coffee's good here. You want some?"

Dottie removed her scarf and sat down. Her eyes were bright and mischievous. "Yes, please."

Bear caught the eye of their waiter and ordered two more coffees.

When he left, Bear leaned back as best he could and folded his hands over his stomach.

"How have you been? Keeping dry?"

"Oh, you know. Best as I can." Dottie smiled and pushed a piece of hair out of her face. "And you? It's been some time, Mr. Logan. We don't see you over here too often."

"I was actually just here about a week ago. Business keeps me coming back, I guess."

"And how are you enjoying your time so far?"

Bear held back his answer as the waiter delivered their coffees. They both declined ordering breakfast. When the man walked away, Bear returned his attention to Dottie.

"It's been a little quiet for my liking," Bear said. "I'm trying to track down a friend."

"So you said in your message." Dottie looked at Bear over the rim of her mug as she took a sip. When she set it back down on the table, she looked serious. "Is Jack okay?"

"That's what I'm trying to find out. I haven't heard from him in a while."

"That's not unusual sometimes, though, is it?"

Bear took a sip of his coffee. The heat sliding down his esophagus relaxed and reinvigorated him at the same time. "Depends. Sometimes he disappears for a while. He usually tells me. He told me before he went away this last time."

"Then what has you so worried?"

Bear took a deep breath. This was the moment of truth. He was either going to trust Dottie or he wasn't. She was Jack's contact, someone he had worked with a few times in the past. Bear had met her once or twice, but their interactions had been brief.

Still, in that time, Bear felt like he'd gotten a sense of her. He trusted her, probably because Jack did, but there was still something that made him a little uneasy. He chalked it up to the fact that she was a British operative. She had secrets to hide, like they all did. That didn't make her any less trustworthy. In fact, it made her the right person to keep this inquiry quiet.

He leaned in a little further. "Do you know anyone by the name of Daniel Thorne?"

Dottie looked down at the table like she was trying to read something invisible in front of her. Her eyes moved back and forth, like she was skimming through all of her memory files in a matter of seconds. "Doesn't ring a bell," she said, slowly. "Context?"

"American. Don't know much about his operations, but he's clearly been around for a while. He's made waves but toes the line."

Dottie laughed. "Sure you're not talking about Jack?"

Bear couldn't help but smile. "Fair point."

"I'm sorry, I don't think I've come across him before. Or if I have, it's possible he was using an alias."

Bear nodded. "It was a long shot. Here's another question. Have you heard about a group of CIA operatives stationed in London disappearing off the map?"

Dottie twisted her mouth. "No, but that's not surprising. You Americans don't share as much as you say you do. And neither do my superiors."

"You mind looking into that for me? Finding what you can hear through the grapevine?"

"Sure." Dottie tilted her head to the side. "But what does this have to do with Jack?"

"To be honest, maybe nothing." Bear dragged a hand down his face. "But Thorne has been a pain in our ass for a while now. CIA took him in a week or two ago, and his last words were about Jack."

"What'd he say?"

"How's Jack?" Bear repeated. "Have you heard from him lately?"

Dottie drained her mug. "Not much to go on."

"I didn't think much of it, but I tried to find him anyway. Looked everywhere. Even here. No signs. Nothing. Jack always leaves a trail for me, unless—"

"Unless something's wrong."

Bear nodded. "I'm not saying it's anything. Maybe he's sitting on some beach drinking out of coconut shells and learning how to surf."

"Doesn't really sound like the Jack I know." Dottie laughed. "And he would've told you if he was just taking a vacation."

"My thoughts exactly."

"I'll see what I can find. Jack's always been clever. If he doesn't want to be found, you'll never catch him. But I'll at least ask around. Quietly."

"I appreciate that, Dottie. And if Jack's in trouble, I know he'll appreciate it, too."

"Let's just hope it's the kind of trouble you can get him out of, Mr. Logan."

Bear slid a piece of paper across the table. "My number. In case you do find anything."

Dottie slipped it into her pocket and stood. Bear didn't even attempt to get up this time. It was a lost cause. They said their verbal goodbyes and Bear let Dottie leave first. He paid the bill and waited ten more minutes as a courtesy before exiting the restaurant.

Even if no one was watching, it didn't mean no one would notice. It was better not to be seen together.

CHAPTER SEVEN

With Dottie on the case, Bear's next logical step was to check the address Mr. Jones had provided. He had some other contacts he could get in touch with if the occasion called for it, but too many hands in the cookie jar meant something was bound to break.

So instead, he made his way to the address he had committed to memory the night before. The place the agents had been staying was in an area of Camden that Bear had never been to before. It was obvious why the operatives had chosen this place in particular: it was easy to keep a low profile.

And that's exactly what *he* did. He wound his way down several roads, avoiding the one that housed the apartment building. He wanted to get a feel for the area and a general map of it in his head. If he had to make a quick getaway, this information would be invaluable.

Plus, it was a good way to see if he was being followed.

Once he was happy with the mental map he'd created, and was sure no one was stalking him, Bear walked down the same block the apartment was sitting on. It was a modest building, made of dirty bricks and tiny windows. It was utterly ordinary, neither the best nor the worst building on the block.

It was clear these agents hadn't wanted to be noticed. It was only their regular schedule and Mr. Jones' keen eye that had given them away. Although, Bear couldn't be sure someone else hadn't picked up their scent, either. Had they moved on to another area, unsanctioned, or had their mission been permanently cut short?

Bear made two passes before he found a pub down the street and made himself comfortable. It'd be much easier to keep an eye on the place once the sun went down. He could blend into the shadows. See who frequented the building. Try to figure out what the hell this could have to do with Jack.

Bear ordered another Fuller's and sat in a corner where he could watch the patrons of the bar and the street outside. It was a modest pub, with plenty of locals chatting loudly about whatever was on TV. Bear didn't bother looking. Instead, he had his nose buried in his phone.

Dottie had messaged him to say she'd put the word out. Nothing yet, but she had high hopes. So did Bear. Dottie was one of the most well-connected contacts he and Jack had. If these agents had anything to do with Jack, Dottie would at least be able to help him start connecting the dots. Once he had a thread, he'd follow it as far as he could go.

Until then, all he could do was wait.

Sadie checked in once, but she didn't have any news either. Bear passed the time drinking and making a mental note of who else was in the area that he could reach out to. Then he crossed off everyone he couldn't trust with information about Jack's possible disappearance. It didn't make for a long list.

"You waiting for someone?"

Bear looked up to find the waitress switching out his empty beer bottle for a full one. She didn't seem worried about the idea that he had been there for hours.

"Nah." He lifted the new beer in thanks. "Just thinking."

She nodded her head knowingly. "That's the kind of thing that gets people in trouble."

"That it does."

When it looked like he wasn't going to offer up any more information, she knocked her knuckles on his table. "Well, let me know if you need anything to wash your beer down with."

He gave her a small smile. "Thanks, I will."

Beyond that, no one said anything to Bear, and by the time he'd had three more beers, he was ready to take a closer look at the apartment building. It was dark and the streets had cleared out for the most part. He'd probably fit right in with anyone willing to hang around after hours. His whole mouth tasted like beer, which meant he probably smelled like it too, but he had been drinking slowly enough to keep his mind from being clouded.

The air had chilled since he'd been outside last. He stuck his hands in his pockets and hiked his shoulders up around his ears. He kept his eyes down but made sure to stay aware of everything that crossed through his peripheral vision.

The apartment building wasn't particularly tall, not like they were in New York City, but he counted six stories and four windows across the front. There'd likely be a basement too, and at least fifty apartments.

Just as he was debating the best way to work his way through the building without causing suspicion, he noticed a young boy, maybe eleven or twelve, running straight for him. He had on a dirty jacket and a knit cap, but his sneakers looked bright against the night. Stolen.

The kid didn't slow down as he barreled toward him, so Bear angled his body and planted his feet. Not that it would've mattered. The kid was skin and bones. Still, the action had the desired effect. When the boy hit Bear, he bounced off and fell down, spread eagle on the concrete. Bear looked like he'd been hit by a leaf passing in the wind.

Sure enough, when Bear looked down, the kid was clutching Bear's wallet to his chest.

"You rely on speed too much." Bear grabbed the kid's arm to simultaneously help him up and keep him in place. "You need to be more subtle."

"Let me go!" The kid's voice was just a squeak. "I'll scream."

Bear grabbed his wallet back, but didn't let go of the boy's arm. "Or you can earn this money instead of stealing it."

The boy stilled and looked up at Bear. He seemed suspicious. "How?"

Bear let the kid go and hooked a thumb over his shoulder. "I need you to go in there and tell me everything you see. I want to know what it looks like, what kind of people are inside, if you see anything weird."

"Weird?" The boy didn't talk much, but there was a hint of an Irish accent. "Weird how?"

"You'll know it when you see it." Bear knew what kids like this had to deal with on a daily basis. They had an innate sort of alarm for danger inside of them. "Anything that feels off or wrong, I want to know about it."

The boy crossed his arms and stood up taller. "How much do I get?"

"Fifty pounds," Bear said. "And we'll get takeout too."

The boy's eyes lit up. "Deal."

Bear could practically hear the kid's stomach growl. "You got a name?"

"Seamus."

"Bear."

"Bear?" The boy laughed. "What kind of name is that?"

"It's what my friends call me."

Seamus smiled. "Okay then, Bear. What kind of takeout are we getting?"

"I'm in the mood for some Thai. That good with you?" He'd

spotted a stand around the corner when he was doing his sweeps earlier.

Seamus nodded. "Good with me."

CHAPTER EIGHT

B ear had to force Seamus not to eat all his noodles in one sitting. He was worried they'd come right back up if the kid had to climb six flights of stairs. The boy looked sad as he watched Bear close the lid on his takeout container, but he wiped his hands on his jacket, pulled his cap down over his ears, and made his way back up the street toward the apartment building.

This was the worst part of the job sometimes. The waiting. The cautiousness. Sometimes Bear wanted to employ the *Jack Noble method* and just barrel his way into a situation, guns blazing, and come out the hero every time. Jack had a knack for that kind of shit. But Bear was a bigger target. Best case scenario, he'd end up with a bullet in his ass. Worst case scenario, Jack would have to come out of hiding to attend his funeral.

Then at least Bear would know where he was.

He checked his phone again. No new messages. Wouldn't it be ironic if, after all this trouble, Jack just decided to text him out of the blue? *Hey, Bear, what's up? Mexico is great this time of year. I'm beginning to think I'm addicted to strawberry-banana margaritas. How've you been?*

Bear would tear him a new one.

But daydreaming wasn't going to solve the mystery of the missing agents and it definitely wasn't going to help him track down Jack. So Bear finished off his noodles, threw money down on the table, and grabbed Seamus's leftovers.

He decided to do another circuit around the block before he found a perch where he could watch the building. There were a couple of fire escapes on surrounding buildings that would allow him to get up high and keep an eye out for Seamus exiting.

Except Bear didn't get that far.

As he was crossing in front of the building, a pair of women who could've been sisters burst out the front door. One of them had a baby swaddled against her chest, and the other was desperately trying to keep up.

"Clara, Clara, calm down." The second woman was trying to pull Clara to a stop, but she was like a freight train. "Everything is fine. Let's go back inside."

"No, no, no." Clara was practically in hysterics. "It's been getting worse every day. Someone's died in there. I know it. And if I don't get Benji out, we're going to die, too."

"You're being paranoid, Clara. Really. The baby's going to catch cold out here. I didn't smell anything."

"I know it. I know it." Clara's eyes darted around wildly. She almost ran into Bear, but he doubted she saw him at all. "Smells like death and decay. I know it."

The other woman sidestepped Bear to keep up with her sister, but Bear was no longer concerned about them. He turned his attention to the building, and just looking at its imposing façade filled him with dread. It had been stupid to send Seamus in there. He had no idea what waited for the kiddo. For all he knew, whoever made the agents disappear was waiting for someone to collect them. If Seamus had found the right apartment, he could be walking into a trap.

Bear barreled into the building, taking the stairs two at a time. Seamus hadn't been in there long, so chances were he'd only be on the first few floors. Once he found him, he'd send him on his way and Bear would finish searching the rest of the building by himself.

Everything about the building was old. The stairs, the rugs, the walls. And the stains each held. It was like stepping back in time where everything was muted and tinged with brown. How anyone could keep hope alive living in a place like this was beyond Bear. No wonder the woman with the baby was looking for any excuse to get out.

But soon enough he realized it wasn't an excuse. He'd smelled death enough times that he could recognize the faintest hint of it in the air, and as soon as he hit the second-floor landing, the hair on the back of his neck stood on end.

He pulled his gun from his belt and kept it pointed at the floor. He assumed most people were home at this time of night, and he didn't want to raise suspicions. But everything in his body told him something was wrong and the only thing that made him feel better was having his sidearm ready.

When he stepped into the second-floor hallway, he noticed two doors open on his left. The first must have belonged to the two sisters. There were toys strewn everywhere and a box of diapers sat next to the door. The two of them must've left in such a hurry that they'd forgotten to even close up. Bear shut the door to keep the other residents from taking anything.

The next open door was where the odor was coming from. It was no wonder the young mother had smelled it, and soon enough everyone on this floor would know someone had died. Bear figured the smell had been contained with the door closed, but now that it was cracked, the stench permeated the rest of the hallway.

Bear toed open the door and raised his pistol to chest level. Just because he knew someone had been dead inside for a few days didn't mean there wasn't someone else alive. But he needed to move quickly. If he was caught at the scene and it looked like he was involved, that would add a whole new problem to the long list Sadie was already keeping track of. Neither one of them needed that.

When he reached the end of the short hall into the apartment, he took in the living room but kept moving forward. It was a mess of takeout containers and beer bottles. The place smelled stale, on top of the odor of a dead body. Whoever had been living here hadn't left in quite some time, even before they had died.

Bear cleared the kitchen and made his way to the back bedroom. His heart stopped when he noticed a pair of tiny legs laying across the threshold of the doorway. Seamus was lying face down on the dirty carpet. His eyes were closed and he wasn't moving.

Bear's chest tightened and he couldn't breathe until he knelt down and checked the boy's pulse. When he noticed there was a solid beat to it, Bear allowed himself to exhale. The kid was knocked out cold, but he was alive. But that didn't answer the question of what the hell had happened here.

He'd noticed the dead body as soon as he had walked into the room. It was sitting up in bed, leaned back against the wall. The man had sandy hair and a matching mustache. He was gray and the stench of death was rolling off him in thick waves. There was a single bullet hole in his forehead.

Bear walked deeper into the room, first clearing the bathroom and then making sure no one was hiding in the closet. There was no one else in the apartment. Then what had happened to Seamus?

Bear bent down to the kid to take a closer look and noticed he had a lump on his forehead. Someone had taken him by surprise and then gotten the hell out. But if the man in the bed had been dead for days already, why was someone else in the apartment? And who were they? They clearly hadn't wanted to kill a kid, but they also had no problem knocking him unconscious.

Now that his heartbeat was returning to normal and the blood wasn't pounding in his ears, Bear picked up on a quiet hissing coming from the living room. The smell of death had covered up the stench of something else, and now he noticed how lightheaded he felt.

Sure enough, when Bear went to investigate, he found the culprit in the kitchen. The gas line had been pulled free from the stove.

CHAPTER NINE

Instinct took over. Bear grabbed Seamus in his arms and took off down the hallway, pulling the fire alarm in the process. He kicked open the door to the stairwell, taking it off one of its hinges. He bounded down the steps coming close to snapping an ACL when he missed one. He wasn't sure how long the gas had been leaking into the apartment, but he wasn't going to put the kid in any more danger than he already had. Hopefully everyone inside the building didn't think they could just ignore the alarm.

Part of him wished he could go back inside to look at the apartment for clues, but with his luck, someone would strike a match and the whole building would go up in flames right as he found out what had happened to the guy who'd had his brains blown out.

Instead, he'd have to wait for the fire department and the local police to show up and take care of the situation. Once the gas leak was fixed, maybe Sadie could pull some strings and get him back in there before the scene was trampled.

But first, Bear had to make sure the kid was all right.

He pushed the main door open, not realizing how good the fresh air tasted until he took a deep breath of it. The stench in the apartment had been rancid. He was sure it'd take days to fully remove it from his nostrils, but the cool April breeze was a start.

Bear walked to the corner of the building and sat Seamus down on a bench. The boy was starting to come to, his eyebrows knitting together and a small groan escaping his lips. Bear didn't want the kid to feel scared, so he knelt down in front of him and tried not to look too worried.

"You okay, kid?" Bear was aware of how gruff his voice sounded. Maybe he'd breathed in more of that gas than he thought.

Seamus looked around, left to right, and finally landed on Bear. "What happened?"

"What do you remember?"

"Going inside the building and then upstairs." Seamus's voice sounded stronger the more he talked. He looked up at the building. "There was nothing weird on the first floor, but as soon as I opened the door to the second floor, I smelled... something."

Bear was aware of the people pouring out of the building now, but he ignored them. Tried to keep Seamus's attention fixed forward. "What do you remember smelling?"

Seamus's eyes welled up, but he never let the tears fall. His voice remained steady. "Something bad. Like someone who was dying. Or was already dead."

"Have you smelled something like that before?"

Seamus looked away and nodded.

Bear couldn't imagine everything this child had gone through, and he was maybe twelve years old. He needed a lucky break, but Bear couldn't give it to him at that moment. He needed the full story first. "What next?"

"One of the doors was open a little bit and I could tell the smell was coming from there, so I went inside." He took a deep breath. "It smelled funny inside. Bad, like death, but also sweet. It made my head fuzzy."

"Did you pass out?"

Seamus shook his head, but then thought better of the motion.

His face paled, but he continued anyway. "I heard someone inside, so I was quiet. I'm good at sneaking up on people and hiding. But they caught me."

Bear felt his brain working overtime. Who could've gotten out of the apartment that quickly without his noticing? He would've passed them on the stairs, which meant they went up instead of down. Were they a resident in the building, returning to their own apartment? Or did they know Bear was out there, watching the front entrance?

"Who caught you?" Bear asked.

"A man. I heard him in the bathroom, so I tried to get closer. That's when I noticed the man in the bed."

"Was he already dead?"

Seamus nodded. "The man came out of the bathroom and saw me. He grabbed me by the arm. When I tried to get away, he hit me on the head."

Bear tilted Seamus's face to look at the darkening bruise across his temple. "You're going to be okay."

Seamus looked toward the people gathered around the front of the building. Sirens wailed in the distance. "What happened?"

"There's a gas leak inside. That was the sweet smell you noticed." Bear scratched at his beard. "Do you remember what the man looked like?"

Seamus nodded. "Bald. Brown eyes. He had a beard. He was tall."

"If you looked at some pictures, would you be able to recognize him?"

Seamus's eyes filled with tears again. "You're gonna make me talk to the cops, aren't you?"

Bear sighed. "I know you probably don't want to—"

"I'm gonna get in trouble." Seamus was crying now. "I tried to steal from you and I broke into that apartment."

"You're not in trouble." Bear placed a reassuring hand on the kid's shoulder and it nearly engulfed his whole arm. "Everyone's just going to be happy you're safe, okay?"

Seamus nodded, but Bear had the distinct impression that the boy didn't believe him.

"I have a friend who's going to help you." Bear pulled out his phone and brought up Sadie's number. She had landed late last night. He wasn't sure if he'd be waking her up, but he doubted she'd complain given the situation. "She's the best, and she's going to make sure everyone is really nice to you, okay?"

Seamus nodded. He looked like he wanted to run away, but Bear could tell he was exhausted.

"If you remember anything else, you make sure you tell me or you tell her, okay?"

"Okay." Seamus looked down at his hands and back up at Bear again. "There was something else, too."

"Something else you remember?"

"Yeah." Seamus wiped his nose on his coat sleeve. "The man had a tattoo on his arm. It looked like a dog in a hat. And there were some letters underneath, but they were kind of fancy and I couldn't read them."

Bear froze. "Do you know what kind of dog it was?"

"One of those short dogs with the funny faces. It had lots of teeth."

Bear decided to test Seamus. "Like a Pitbull? Or a Rottweiler?"

"No, it was... a bulldog! Definitely a bulldog. I've seen them before. My cousin Georgie found one once, but it belonged to this old man who shouted at us when we tried to pet him."

Bear didn't waste any time dialing Sadie's phone number. He needed to know what the hell was going on. He needed to know why a member of the United States Marine Corps was in London killing off CIA operatives.

But the second Sadie answered her phone, everything went to shit. A colossal boom nearly knocked Bear off his feet. The apartment building erupted into flames.

CHAPTER TEN

"You saved a lot of lives here today," Sadie said, placing a gentle hand on Bear's shoulder. "There's nothing else you could've done."

Bear looked at the charred building in front of him and grunted. Was the burnt smell coming from across the street? Or had his beard been singed? He didn't feel like a hero. He almost got a kid killed and lost a lot of evidence in the process. And he wasn't any closer to figuring out what the hell was going on here either.

"Seriously." Sadie forced Bear to look at her by placing her face in front of his. He focused on her. "You did your best."

"I know, I know," Bear said. He wiped the sweat off his forehead with the back of his arm, no doubt replacing it with a streak of soot in the process.

As soon as the building had exploded, Bear instructed Seamus to stay put and launched himself toward the entrance. People were running and screaming in all directions, still filing out the door. He shouted the address into his phone, hoping Sadie caught it before he hung up and gave the people in front of him all his attention.

It had been a couple minutes since Bear had pulled the fire alarm, so most everyone had exited the building. The only ones left were some of the older residents, a few of which were still making their way down the stairs, moving as quickly as they could. Some clutched a cat or a dog to their chest. Bear carefully helped them to the door until the stream of people stopped altogether.

He couldn't be sure no one else was inside, but the fire had quickly spread from the single apartment to the entire second story, and the smoke thickened to the point he couldn't see the stairwell anymore. He did a sweep of the first floor, ensuring everyone had gotten out, but he couldn't even get the door open on the landing above without burning the skin off his hand.

Instead, Bear made sure everyone outside remained calm and those who had any injuries were resting and drinking water that someone from an adjacent building had brought over. The crowd grew by the minute as the flames continued to expand, having broken through the windows at the front and sides of the structure.

The fire department showed up ten minutes later. Sadie was there shortly after. It took them about an hour to put it out and give the all-clear for the authorities to make their way in and search for evidence, even with smoke still swirling in the air.

"What's the news?" Bear asked. He appreciated her trying to make him feel better, but he needed information more than condolences.

"The fire alarm was enough to clear out the first four floors. Those people would be dead if you hadn't pulled it. There were some people left on the top couple floors, but the fire department got here before the damage could spread too far."

"A lot of people still lost everything today."

"But they kept their lives." Sadie's voice was stern. "And as terrible as this might be for them, I know they're all grateful for that."

It didn't make Bear feel much better. He needed more than that. "What about evidence?"

"Everything in the apartment you were in is charred. We have evidence of bones, which I'm assuming is the guy in the bed that you mentioned, but we won't know his identity for a while longer. Any other physical evidence has likely been destroyed."

"I WONDER WHAT IGNITED THE GAS. I DIDN'T SEE ANYTHING that could've caused a spark. Nothing was hot in the apartment. Everyone on that floor who could've caused it to go up vacated when I pulled the alarm."

"Maybe someone didn't stub out their cigarette in the next apartment. We'll probably never know."

"Yeah, probably."

Bear could feel Sadie's stare on his face.

"You've got another theory," she said.

"What if the perp never left the building? He could've gone up a flight of stairs and come back down after the floor was clear."

"And got out of there before it exploded?"

"You know it's possible. Seamus said the guy was a marine."

"Seamus said this?"

"The tattoo he described. Anyway, this isn't some civilian causing trouble. He wanted that evidence gone. Didn't have a problem hurting a little kid, possibly even leaving him to die."

Sadie paced along the sidewalk. "Let's say you're right. He gets caught by the kid, knocks him out and then panics, thinking Seamus might not be by himself. He runs upstairs to get away, and then hears the fire alarm. Figures that's his best bet to clean up his mess. Waits a few minutes, goes back down, and sets the place on fire. Goes out the window or a back staircase."

Bear shrugged. "It's definitely possible."

Sadie shook her head. "Maybe that's how it played out, but that's not the whole story."

"How do you figure?"

"You said that agent reeked." She gestured to the building behind her. "He'd been dead a few days, maybe even a week at that point. The weather's been cool."

"And?"

"Whoever killed that guy could've cleared out the apartment when they did the deed. Could've set the whole thing ablaze and been done with it. The trail would've been colder by the time we had gotten to it."

"You think someone set a trap?"

Sadie nodded. "They wanted someone to pick up the scent before they destroyed it."

"Which means—"

"Someone knows what we're up to," Sadie finished. "Someone's watching us."

CHAPTER ELEVEN

Sadie didn't waste any time high-tailing it out of there. She and Bear hopped into her car, and she floored it out of the city. Seamus had been moved to a safe house in the suburbs an hour or two prior, and that was the next stop on their list. The whole situation wasn't sitting right with either one of them, and he was the only one who had come close to their mysterious Marine.

It took a good forty-five minutes to put London behind them, and then another half hour to find their way to a cozy little residential area that looked like it had never seen an exciting day in its life. The perfect place for a secret government hideout.

As soon as Sadie pulled past the tall hedges and into the driveway, two agents with concealed weapons approached them and opened their doors.

A man with a flattop opened the driver's side door, gave them both a nod. "Ma'am. Sir."

Sadie got out of the car and surveyed their surroundings. "Everything been quiet?"

"Yes, ma'am," Flattop answered. "Nothing to report."

"Bhandari's inside?"

"Yes, ma'am."

Sadie motioned for Bear to follow her, and the two of them made their way up the front steps and inside the modest house. From the outside, it looked like it was primed for a small family of three or four. There would be enough room for the kids to be kids, but it didn't seem like it would break the bank, either. Bear absently wondered what the cover story was. Neighbors were nosy, after all.

They were met at the door by a tall, lean, Indian man with gelled hair and a smile that was a little too perfect. His stubble was artfully trimmed, and a pair of dimples told Bear he probably had no trouble in the relationship department. The only imperfection on his face was a small scar that traveled out from the corner of his left eye. Then again, that probably only added to his allure.

"Good to see you," he said, shaking Sadie's hand. Then, turning to Bear and doing the same, "Mr. Logan. It's a pleasure to meet you. I apologize for the excitement the two of you had today. London's best viewed when it's not on fire."

Bear chuckled. He liked this guy's dark sense of humor, but he sobered quickly. "How's the kid?"

Bhandari's face tightened. "Frightened. Took a minute to get him to relax enough to eat. We got him cleaned up and put him in some new clothes. But he hasn't been saying much. Kept asking for you, though."

"Mind if we talk with him for a few?" Sadie asked.

"Please," Bhandari said, gesturing for the pair of them to go before him.

Bear followed Sadie down the hallway and into a small living room. It was furnished, but the plain sofa and chair, the small TV, and the single end table left a lot to be desired. There were no pictures on the walls. All the curtains were drawn. The ceiling light in the middle of the room cast a yellow glow over everything. It didn't feel like a home at all.

Seamus was curled up on the couch, knees to his chest, staring off into space. When the group entered the room, Bear could see him visibly relax. He sat up and crossed his legs, looking expectantly up at them. Bear couldn't help but notice how much younger he looked without all the dirt on his face.

"You okay, kid?" Bear asked. "They treating you right?"

"Yeah," Seamus replied. He sounded forlorn. "Gave me some new clothes. And new shoes."

Bear looked to where he was pointing. In the corner of the room were a pair of pretty simple sneakers, blue with red stripes. That was bragging rights when you were a homeless kid. Everyone would either want to be his friend or try to take them from him.

"We have some questions for you, kid. Mind if we sit down?"

Seamus shook his head, but he looked nervous again. "Am I in trouble?"

"Not at all," Sadie said. Her voice was calm and even. She had a gentle smile on her face. "You're not going to get into trouble for anything, okay? We just need to know what happened so we can help those people who lost their homes today."

"Okay." Seamus's voice sounded so small. "Is everyone okay?"

Bear sat down next to Seamus. "Yeah, buddy. Everyone's okay. We just want to figure out what happened."

"I already told you everything I know."

"Do you mind telling me, too?" Sadie asked. "Maybe I'll be able to think of something Bear couldn't."

Bear shot her an incredulous look and Seamus laughed. It was quick, but it was enough. Sadie had already won him over. He told her exactly what he'd told Bear, from the minute he got to the second floor to when he woke up outside with Bear hovering over him.

"Did the man speak to you at all?" Sadie asked.

Seamus shook his head.

"That tattoo you saw means that man was in the Marines. Do you know who the Marines are?"

Seamus shook his head again.

"It means that he was American, like me and Bear." She paused and shifted slightly closer to Seamus. "Have you met any Americans before?"

"Just the ones we try to pickpocket. Tourists. But everyone else is like me."

"English, you mean?"

He nodded. "Or Irish. Or Scottish. My friend Alex moved here from Scotland. Then his mom got locked up and he ran away from his foster home."

Sadie and Bear exchanged looks. Seamus said it like it was matter-of-fact, not like it was a travesty that kids like this were living out their worst nightmares on the streets every night.

"Seamus, did anyone tell you to target Bear specifically?"

Seamus squirmed in his seat.

"Remember, you're not going to get into trouble with us, okay? We're just trying to help. And if you're scared of anyone, we'll make sure they can't hurt you."

"I'm not worried about me," Seamus said. His face went red. "I'm worried about Annie. She's my friend. She might get in trouble, too."

"Why would Annie get into trouble?" Sadie asked.

"She was supposed to make sure I didn't mess up. She's older than me. Smarter and better, too. She was watching to make sure I didn't get in trouble when I tried to pickpocket Bear."

"How come she didn't show up when it didn't work?" Bear asked.

"I gave her a signal. Told her everything was okay. I figured you'd give me money and maybe I'd be able to split some food with her and everything would be okay."

"But you're worried now?"

"I was supposed to take your whole wallet and your phone." Seamus was visibly shaking now. "Usually we just take the money, but she told me to take everything. I was confused because phones can get us in trouble. They can be tracked down. But I always listen to Annie. She looks out for me."

Bear looked over at Sadie. "Sounds like someone wanted to know who I was and what I was up to."

Sadie turned back to Seamus. "Who gave Annie those instructions?"

"I don't know." He looked between Sadie, Bear, and Bhandari. "I'm not allowed to talk to him."

"Why not?" Sadie asked.

"Annie said it's because he's busy. But I think she was just being nice. I think it's because I'm not very good yet. And he only wants to talk to the kids who do a good job."

Bear reached over and ruffled Seamus's hair.

Sadie turned to Bhandari. "Can we try to find this Annie? Make sure she's all right?"

"We sure can." He stood up and smiled down at Seamus. "We'll find her, okay? We'll make sure she doesn't get into trouble."

Just as Bhandari left the room to go make some phone calls, Flattop entered the room, a tablet in one hand and a phone in the other.

"Ma'am, the lineup of the Marines you requested. And you've also got a phone call."

Sadie exchanged a look with Bear. "From who?"

"Headquarters, ma'am." He held out the phone. "They say it's an emergency."

CHAPTER TWELVE

"I got a bad feeling about this," Bear said.

"I don't know why," Sadie replied. "Everything about this situation is completely normal. Look at me. I'm totally at ease."

Bear appreciated the sarcasm, but he couldn't grant her more than a wry smile. Something was definitely off here, but he couldn't figure out what it was. That was the most unsettling part.

Sadie's call with MI5 headquarters was short. They requested that both she and Bear come in voluntarily, to which she agreed. Flattop insisted on driving them himself, and even though he never said, Bear was sure he had been instructed to take them there. For some reason the government wanted to keep tabs on the two of them, and the easiest way to do that was with some traditional English hospitality.

But Bear saw it for what it was.

The drive back into London was quicker than their trip out. Traffic had eased a bit, and Flattop seemed to specialize in high speed chases. His ability to weave safely in and out of traffic was commendable, even if it did earn them more than a few honked horns.

Now Sadie and Bear were being marched down a long hallway in

a government building, accompanied by two armed guards. Flattop
had stayed in the car. Bear already missed him. He didn't say much,
but he was a generally affable kind of guy. Seemed like he'd be fun at
parties once he loosened up a bit. Maybe Bear would buy him a drink
and try to get some stories out of him. He looked like a guy who had a
few good ones up his sleeve.

"I'm totally at ease, too," Bear said. "I could take a nap standing
up. Seriously, I'm half catatonic."

"Well, make sure you stay on your feet because I'm not dragging
your sorry ass down this hallway." She twisted around and looked
behind them. "Seriously, how long is this hallway? It's gotta hold a
record or something."

Bear caught one of the guards smiling. He'd never make it as part
of the Queen's guard.

"Through here," the other agent said, stopping in front of one of
many identical doors. This one was labeled 317C. The door was
metal and had a bolt on the outside.

"Uh, mind telling us what this is about?" Bear asked. He didn't
exactly love the idea of going into a room he couldn't get out of.

"Thank you, gentleman," said a voice from behind him. "I'll take
it from here."

Bear turned to see an older woman with graying hair exiting a
room opposite them. There was an ominous pile of manila folders in
her hand. She wore a white blazer and skirt with a light pink top on
underneath. The whole effect made her look soft and warm, but Bear
didn't miss the sharpness of her eyes. Whoever this was, she was
important.

Sadie held out her hand. "My name is—"

"I know who both of you are," the woman replied. She shook
Sadie's hand and then moved on to Bear. "My name is Charlotte
Winters. I'm sorry to have to summon you like this. I'm sure it's
starting us off on the wrong foot. But there's no time to waste."

"Did we do something wrong?" Bear asked. There was something about this woman that reminded him of his grandmother. He felt like Seamus now, wondering if he was in trouble.

"Not at all." Charlotte opened the door to 317C and entered first, gesturing for them to join her. "In fact, I heard you did quite a few things right today, Mr. Logan. I'm grateful you were able to save those people from that building."

Charlotte sat and Bear and Sadie followed suit. The room was stark white, with a single table, four chairs, and a television screen against the far wall. It felt claustrophobic with the three of them in there. This clearly was not a normal meeting room. The small size could be an interrogation tactic. Anything that made your subject feel uncomfortable could ultimately benefit you in the end. The more uneasy they were, the more likely they'd eventually spill their secrets.

Bear and Sadie exchanged looks while Charlotte organized the files in front of her. When she was satisfied, she folded her hands on top of them and surveyed her guests.

Bear resisted the urge to shift uncomfortably in his seat.

"Ma'am," Sadie said. "If time is limited, don't you think we should get down to business?"

"I'm deciding how much I can trust you," Charlotte said. "Sometimes that takes time."

"We've given you no reason to distrust us," Sadie said. "We've been cooperative. Neither one of us has anything to hide."

"That's not true." Charlotte looked over at Bear. "Mr. Logan has quite a lot that's been scrubbed clean from his records."

"That doesn't mean I'm trying to hide it," Bear said. "It just means I don't want anyone to know about it."

Charlotte chuckled. "A fair distinction in our line of work. To be quite honest with you both, the second I made the call to bring you in, I decided you were trustworthy. I must continue to trust my first instincts."

Bear could tell Sadie was growing impatient, so he jumped in before she could. "What's this about, Agent Winters?"

"*Director* Winters," Charlotte replied. "But I appreciate your formality. This, Mr. Logan, is about the body you found today in the apartment building in Camden. I presume he was your man, Agent Bauer?"

"I believe so, yes." Sadie kept her voice level, factual. "They were here with your government's knowledge. We were working with MI5 to track possible terrorist threats in London. What affects our allies, affects us."

"I am aware." Charlotte's voice was not unkind, but it left little doubt in Bear's mind that she knew just about everything that went on under her nose. "About three weeks ago, your men went radio silent. We were unable to track a single one of them down. Until yesterday."

Sadie nodded. "I found out they were being used for a different operation without my knowledge. That's when I sent Bear—Mr. Logan—over here to find them for me."

Charlotte quirked her eyebrow, but didn't comment on the nickname. "What kind of operation?"

"That's what we're trying to find out," Sadie said. "Perhaps if you shared what you know, we may be able to solve this together."

Charlotte nodded her head and removed a small remote from her jacket pocket. She clicked a button and the television screen lit up. When she clicked another button, a video began to play.

At first the room was dimly lit, like there was a light on somewhere behind the camera, but it could barely reach the far wall. Ten seconds passed. Then twenty. Finally, someone switched on a lamp. The entire room was illuminated. The walls and floor were made of concrete. They were dirty and wet. A faint rustling sound filled the background along with a soft echo, but Bear couldn't quite put his finger on what it was. There was nothing in the frame that could possibly tell them where this video had been shot.

In the center of the room was a single foldout chair. In it sat a man covered in bruises. Blood dripping steadily from somewhere on his face. Impossible to determine due to the trauma he'd suffered. His hands were tied behind his back, but his captors didn't bother tying his legs. One was broken. He wasn't going anywhere.

When the light came on, the man looked up. He squinted against the brightness, blinking over and over again. A tear fell from the corner of his eye, but Bear couldn't tell if it was from the sharpness of the light or from the fear he felt. Either way, Bear recognized the agent. It was the man from the apartment. He looked rough, like someone had been using him as a punching bag for several days.

There was no warning. No lead up. No words spoken. One minute the man was sitting there, looking into the light, and the next there was a bang. The man's head jerked back and then his whole body slumped.

The video went black and Winters hit pause.

Bear felt how stiff Sadie's body was in reaction to what they had just seen. He turned to Director Winters. "That's it?"

"That's just the first part," she said. "But I'd like to hear your take on it."

"They didn't announce who they were or what they wanted," Bear said. "They just shot him."

"It was a show of strength." Sadie's voice was tight. Angry. "A warning shot."

Bear scoffed. "This wasn't a warning shot. It was an execution."

"They wanted us to take them seriously," Sadie said. She turned to Winters. "I'm assuming they sent another video."

"They did."

"Wait a minute," Bear interrupted. "This isn't where we found him. That means he was killed and then moved. His body had been staged."

"How could they have moved him back into the apartment?" Sadie asked. "Someone must've seen them."

Charlotte shrugged. "Late at night when the only people out on the streets are either drunk or homeless? Someone probably did see something, but they either wouldn't remember or wouldn't want to share."

"What about people in the building?" Bear asked.

"They only had to take him to the second floor. And if it was in the middle of the night, most people would be asleep."

"You'd either have to be very lucky or very good to coordinate that," Bear said.

"My thoughts exactly." Charlotte raised the remote again. "We received that video ten days ago. The second video came in this morning."

She pressed play and the black screen switched back to the same view, but everything was different. Instead of the chair, there was a Middle Eastern man standing in the middle of the room. His face was mostly covered by a scarf, but his skin was deeply tanned and bits of his beard stuck out here and there.

Behind him were the two missing agents. They were kneeling, their hands tied behind their backs. They also looked like someone had made them their punching bags. The one on the left was barely conscious, hardly able to hold himself up. The other stared straight ahead, but his eyes were vacant. It didn't look like he was scared. It looked like he had given up.

"We have executed one of your men already," said the man in the center. "The other two will follow in three days' time if you do not meet our demands. The United Kingdom and the United Kingdom's allies have imprisoned five men. You will release them immediately. If you do not, these men will be executed. If you continue to refuse us, we will continue to kill your men."

The man took a step closer to the screen. "We will not stop until we have justice. Release Josiah Scott, Anthony Temple, Georges Andrews, Dymek Antar, and Elijah Nowak. You will receive instructions in seventy-two hours."

The video went black seconds later, but not before the man on the right, the one who was staring straight ahead, looked directly into the camera. There was finally fear in his eyes. He didn't say anything, but Bear knew exactly what he was doing.

He was pleading for his life.

CHAPTER THIRTEEN

"Who are those men?" Sadie asked. She was all business now. A fire ignited within her.

"We haven't been able to find any connection between them. Two are being held in the United States. Three of them are here in London. A white supremacist, a drug dealer, an abuser, a car thief, and a sex trafficker. As far as we know, they have no connection to one another."

"They must." Sadie put her hands on the table and leaned forward. "Why else would they ask for those five specifically?"

"At this point, your guess is as good as mine," Winters said. "We're looking into it now. I've also put in a call with your superiors. If there's a connection, someone will find it. I told them to contact you directly if they find out anything."

"Could Thorne be a part of this?" Bear asked Sadie.

Charlotte's attention snapped to him. "Who's Thorne?"

Sadie didn't look happy that his name was now on the table, but Bear had made an executive decision. Winters could have easily gone over their heads and kept them in the dark, but she had no interest in peacocking and neither did he. The sooner they figured this out, the sooner he'd be able to find Jack.

Sadie said, "Thorne is the man who decided my agents were going to do his bidding." She turned to Bear. "But I don't think so. When I first told him they were missing, he was livid. I've never seen him that out of control before."

"He's a good actor. He had all of us fooled for a while," Bear said.

"Look, I'm not discounting the possibility. It's a thread to follow. But I have a feeling it's going to lead to a dead end."

"I think we need to have a chat with Maria," Bear said. And before she could ask, he turned to Winters and explained. "She was Thorne's protégé. She fed the agents intel she thought was credible. Turns out she thought wrong."

"We need to figure out where she got that intel," Charlotte said.

"And from whom," Sadie finished.

Winters walked to the door and called out to one of her men. Within ten minutes, there was a fancy laptop sitting in front of Bear and he was video chatting with Maria. Sadie was seated next to him, but Director Winters was behind the computer. They all thought it better not to chance Maria getting spooked if she knew MI5 was involved.

Maria answered on the second ring, holding her phone out in front of her so all Bear could see was her face. Her red hair was in a messy bun and she looked like she had just woken up, even though it was the middle of the afternoon. But as soon as Bear told her they'd found one of the agents dead, she sat up a little straighter.

"Was it because of what I told them?" she asked.

"We don't know for sure," Bear said. "But it's likely. We need to know everything you do."

Maria's hand absently found a loose strand of hair and began twisting it between her fingers. "Like I said, I was trying to clean up loose ends. I was still mad about Thorne. Still pissed that he never really cared about me to begin with. The CIA wanted more information about what he'd been up to, so I decided to backtrack and dig into all my past cases. I wanted to know what had really happened after I was done with a job. Was he telling me the truth? Or was I doing his dirty work and never really knew it?"

"Why'd you start with the three agents?" Sadie asked.

Maria shrugged. "It was one of the more recent jobs I'd done before Korea. And it was all informational. I didn't have to do anything more than survey targets and then pass along anything interesting I saw. None of it seemed connected at the time, but I figured if I started looking back on it, maybe a bigger picture would form."

Bear tipped the screen down so he could see her a little better. "And did it?"

"Not really." Maria sighed. "To be honest, I didn't get very far either. I found out they were missing and figured I was in over my head. That's when I reached out to you."

Bear turned to Sadie. "And you knew about the missing agents before Maria stumbled across them?"

Sadie said, "Of course I did. They were my men. We'd already been working on finding them. The project with Maria was unrelated. Until it wasn't."

In other words, Bear thought, until they realized Thorne had probably stuck his nose where it didn't belong. Bear returned his attention to Maria.

"Let's talk about this last piece of information you passed on to the agents. What was it? Why do you think it was bad intel?"

"Well, they'd gone missing, didn't they?" Maria seemed annoyed, but Bear thought it was more at herself than either one of them. "The intel was stupid. Harmless. Even in the moment it didn't seem like vital life-or-death information, you know?"

"Start at the beginning," Sadie said. Her patience was immaculate on the surface, but Bear could tell the runaround was starting to get to her. All this paper chasing was driving him crazy, too. He was ready to start shooting things again.

"I had been in London for a couple weeks at that point. I had been gathering intel a couple different ways. Sometimes it was an envelope slipped under my door. Sometimes it was a phone call. I'd be given a time and a place, and I was to arrive an hour beforehand to start scoping the area. I'd set myself up somewhere comfortable, and then I'd just wait and watch."

"How did you receive the information this time?" Bear asked.

"Phone call. Anonymous, like always. It was always a guy on the other end of the phone, but sometimes the voices were different. I wasn't sure if I had multiple people calling me or if they used a voice modulator. Or, for that matter, maybe all the information was coming from one person and they just employed multiple people to deliver it."

"That didn't seem a little unorthodox to you?" Bear asked. It's not like he hadn't taken an anonymous phone call once or twice in his life, but they usually led to disaster. He tried to know who was passing him information, if only to cover his own ass.

Maria laughed. "Doesn't Thorne seem a little unorthodox to you? But no. This was how it was done. My job was to trust Thorne one hundred percent of the time. And I did. No questions asked."

"What did the anonymous caller sound like?" Sadie asked.

"Male. American. Deep voice. Maybe a twinge of a Southern accent, but if so, he was doing a damn good job of covering it up. Polite. Kind of sexy, to be honest."

Bear cleared his throat. "Focus."

"Don't be a prude, Bear. He sounded like a pretty typical, all-American boy." She tilted her head back and looked up at the ceiling like she was deep in thought. "He told me about a terrorist cell in London. There had been reports of so-called accidents all around the city. Little tests for response time, crowd reactions, things like that."

Charlotte sat up a little straighter at the mention of a terrorist cell, but she remained silent on the other side of the computer.

"And you just believed him?" Bear asked. "What if he'd been lying?"

Maria said, "I know I'm relatively new at this, but I'm not an idiot. I looked into it. Pulled up the newspapers on my computer. Everything checked out. He told me when the next one was going to take place. Gave me an address. I was supposed to stay clear of the area but take note of everyone who passed through. Then pass that information on."

"What happened when you got there?"

"A restaurant caught fire. I took some pictures and passed them along to the agents. I thought they might be able to recognize someone."

"Did they?" Bear asked.

Maria twisted up her face. "Like they'd tell me. I dropped off the information and I left, just like always. That wasn't a two-way street."

"Did anything feel wrong about the job at the time?" Sadie asked.

"Nope. Pretty straightforward. One of the easier ones, actually. Everything happened like the informant said it would."

"And it didn't bother you that this person knew this information and instead of going to the authorities with it, he gave it to you? Just so you could watch?" Sadie asked.

"My job," Maria said, her voice tight, "was to trust Thorne one-hundred percent of the time. Besides, I figured it was for the greater good."

Sadie just barely kept her scoff to herself. "How so?"

"If sitting by and letting this accident happen meant we could put an end to a terrorist cell, it would be worth it."

"Do you still have the pictures?" Bear asked. Perhaps with the photos they could get somewhere with this case.

Maria shook her head. "I gave them hard copies and deleted the pictures off my phone. Totally scrubbed clean."

Sadie leaned back in her chair. "We'll need you to give us as much information as you can about the articles you researched and the fire you witnessed."

"I remember some of them," Maria said. "It might be enough to put together a pattern."

"Thanks, Maria," Bear said.

"Any time, Bear." Her face grew serious. "Thanks again. For everything. If you need anything else—"

"I know where you are," Bear said. Maria waved goodbye and Bear shut down the computer.

The room was silent for a solid minute. Charlotte was the first to break it.

"How much do you trust this girl?"

Bear and Sadie exchanged looks. Bear opened his mouth to answer, but Sadie beat him to it.

"She's green. Naïve. I'm not convinced she's out from under Thorne's thumb just yet. Whether or not she knows it is a whole other story."

"I want to trust her," Bear said.

"That's not the same thing as saying you do trust her," Charlotte said.

"I know." Bear's sigh felt like it weighed a hundred pounds. "But I'm with Sadie on this one. Thorne's one of the best. Maria only knew what he wanted her to know. I think she means well, but her intel is unreliable."

"Noted." Charlotte stood up and gathered her papers. "But at least we have a place to start now. That's better than nothing."

Bear wanted to agree, but something still felt off about the whole thing. They had a lot of puzzle pieces but none of them fit together. The agents. The terrorist group. The kid and his mysterious boss. Maria and Thorne. Jack's disappearance.

At some point there had to be a thread connecting them all together.

Right?

CHAPTER FOURTEEN

Excuse yourself to go to the bathroom.

E Bear looked at the text on his phone. It took him a second to register what it said. Then another minute to put the pieces together. He was at MI5 headquarters. Dottie must've gotten wind he was here. Maybe she had information on Jack.

While Sadie concluded their meeting with Director Winters, Bear got directions to the closest bathroom and headed down the hall, even deeper into the building's interior. Luckily, the two guards who had brought them in and were still stationed outside the meeting room didn't follow him. What would have been the point? There were cameras everywhere.

Bear pushed opened the door to the bathroom. It was small and tidy. Three stalls and a urinal. Smelled like lemon. It made his nose burn, but it was better than the alternative. There weren't any cameras in here. There couldn't be, legally. But he wondered about listening devices. He didn't want to be the person who had to go over those tapes.

What surprised him most was that the room was empty. He wasn't sure what he was expecting. Dottie lounging on a couch against the wall, a drink in one hand and a cigarette in another? Not exactly, but it would've been a nice welcome party. He could use a drink right about now.

Instead, his phone vibrated. He answered it on the first ring.

"Hello, Bear." Definitely Dottie. "Heard you were in the neighborhood. I'm outside away from listening ears. Try not to say anything too damning, just in case."

"You know I was just wondering about that," Bear said. "Shitty job."

"Literally." Dottie laughed at her own joke. "Luckily that's well below my pay grade."

"You got news?"

"Of sorts." Dottie's voice sobered. "Jack was here, in London, about three weeks ago."

"You're kidding."

"Nope."

"This doesn't feel like good news."

Dottie sighed. "I'm not sure it is. He used one of his many aliases. Almost didn't catch it, but I remembered a few of his go-to ones from back in the day."

"Could be a sign," Bear said. "He could've used anything."

"He's either leaving a trail for us, or he was desperate."

"Either one doesn't bode well." Bear scratched at his chin, deep in thought.

Dottie filled in the blanks. "It means he wants to be found or doesn't care if he is."

"What was on the itinerary?"

"I wish I knew. He came through Heathrow and then disappeared. He hasn't checked into any hotels, booked any plane tickets, used any credit cards. I haven't been able to find him on CCTV, but I'll keep looking."

"You might be wasting your time," Bear said.

"I know. If Jack wants to disappear, he will. And no one will be able to find him." Dottie took a deep breath, and Bear got the distinct feeling she was trying to convince herself as much as him. "But he did want someone to find him. He wanted someone to know he was in London."

"It wasn't supposed to be like this," Bear said. "Disappear. That was the plan."

Something or someone had brought him out of hiding, Bear thought. If Jack had gotten a lead on Thorne, he would've taken it, damn the consequences. If he couldn't find Bear, he would've gone off on his own. Noble was like a pit bull. When he sunk his teeth into something, he was relentless.

But even if Jack couldn't find Bear, he knew where Sadie was. Why didn't he reach out to her? She had proven herself in the field. She was trustworthy. There was definitely something between them. But maybe Jack had assumed, like Bear, that Sadie was happy behind her desk at Langley. It was only after the events in Korea that Bear found out she'd been back in the field much sooner than anyone expected.

Or maybe Jack was trying to protect her. Protect all of them. The revelation that he had landed in London wasn't a mistake, Bear was sure of that. But if he wasn't trying to catch their attention, maybe he was trying to reassure them that he was okay.

But Bear knew one thing for sure. He wasn't about to stop looking based on an assumption. If something else was going on here, Bear needed to know about it. He had to make sure Jack hadn't dug himself too deep into whatever shit he'd gotten in. If Bear found him and Jack told him to fuck off, he'd do just that. But he had to know either way.

"Thanks for the information. I appreciate it."

"I wish I had more. But I'll keep digging. If I find anything else, I'll let you know."

"Sounds good to me." Bear looked around the bathroom. "But I preferred our last talk. At least there was coffee."

Dottie didn't laugh. "One last thing?"

Bear didn't like the hesitance in her voice. "Yeah? What is it?"

"Director Winters is a good woman. A good agent. But she plays things pretty close to her chest."

"You think she's hiding something?" Bear asked.

"I don't think. I know it." Dottie sighed. "I'm not sure what she brought you in on, but rest assured she's only revealing information she absolutely needs to share with you. Anything else she'll keep under wraps until you need to know it."

"You sound like you don't agree with those methods."

Bear could practically hear the shrug in her voice. "To each their own. I trust you because I trust Jack. She doesn't know you. You're a bit of a wild card. You can count on the fact that she's done her homework on you."

"That's been made clear." Bear eyed the door, wondering how much longer he could get away with being in the bathroom before someone came looking for him or an agent happened to walk in to use the facilities.

"I'm not saying don't trust her," Dottie said. "I'm just saying to be cautious. I'm not sure if she knows about Jack or not, but if she does and she's keeping that from you, there might be some sticky situations in your future."

"Understood."

"Bye for now, Bear," Dottie said. "I hope you find Jack soon. I have a bad feeling about this."

"Me too," Bear said. "On both accounts."

CHAPTER FIFTEEN

Bear woke up the next morning to a knock on his door. The night before he'd taken Sadie's advice and changed venues for his sleeping arrangements. They'd gotten a pair of rooms on the same floor in a moderate hotel in the middle of the city. If they were being watched, it was better not to hole up in the same place every night.

Sadie's voice filtered through the closed door as she knocked again. "It's me."

Bear wiped the sleep from his eyes and rolled out of bed. When he answered the door, she looked him up and down with an eyebrow raised. He realized he was only wearing one sock.

"You look like shit," she said.

Sadie, on the other hand, looked like she'd been up for hours. She was wearing a long-sleeved shirt, jeans, and boots. Her hair was tied back and she held both her phone and a tablet in her hands. She looked like she could blend in anywhere in the city.

"Thanks," Bear said. He rooted around in the sheets to find his other sock. "That's the look I was going for."

Sadie didn't entertain the joke. "You want the bad news or the bad news?"

Bear groaned. "Why can't we ever get good news?" He retrieved his sock, put it on, and then walked over to the desk to make them both a cup of terrible coffee. "Let's go with the bad news first."

"Langley called. We have a major problem. Maria's setup was an internal job."

Bear looked at her over his shoulder. "You've got a mole?"

"Looks like it." She sat down and swiped a finger across the screen of her tablet a few times. "They took a look at her computer and went through her search history. All the information the informant told her? Fake."

Bear leaned down to inhale the smell of freshly brewed coffee. It might be hotel coffee, but it'd still get the job done.

"How is that even possible?" he asked. "She verified the intel."

"They planted evidence. When the tech guys followed the trail on her computer, everything showed up just like Maria said. But when they matched it on one of their own, it wasn't there. Doesn't exist."

"They specifically targeted her IP address." Bear poured the first cup of coffee. "Cream? Sugar?"

"One of each," Sadie answered. "And yeah, looks like it."

Bear handed her the coffee. "That seems complicated."

"It is. Or at least, that's what the tech guys tell me. To be honest, they kind of lost me halfway through the explanation, but in order to gain access to her computer like that and build up the evidence to look authentic enough? They were working on it for quite some time."

"What about her phone? Or a library computer? How did they know she'd use her own?"

Sadie shrugged and watched as Bear poured himself a cup of coffee. "Maybe they had backups in place. But her computer would be the most secure device. And if she was constantly looking up information and verifying intel, Thorne probably instructed her to use something they had control over."

"I still think he's in on this somehow," Bear said.

"Maybe." Sadie blew on her coffee. "But he was using Maria to his own ends. He could've found a hundred *straightforward* ways to do this."

"Thorne's good at covering his tracks." Bear ignored the burning of his tongue as he took a sip of his coffee. "And we already know he thinks of Maria as disposable."

"That's fair. I guess we can't rule him out."

"What's the other bad news?" Bear asked.

Sadie set her cup down and swiped her finger across her tablet again. "*Director* Winters reached out again about the five men named in the video."

Bear recalled his conversation with Dottie. "Do you trust her?"

"Winters?" Sadie didn't look up from her tablet. "Yeah, I guess. She seemed to be upfront with us. I appreciated her keeping me in the loop even though she reached out to Langley herself. She didn't need to do that. Why?"

"Just curious. Was there any connection between the men?"

"Hardly anything of significance," Sadie said. "Different crimes, different cities, different arresting officers. Serving different times in different jails. All of them had priors and none of them are close to finishing up their sentence."

"Why would a terrorist organization pick them then? It doesn't make sense."

"Only two of them have any ties to terrorism, and not even the same groups." She finally looked up and locked eyes with Bear. "Maybe we're missing something."

"Or maybe it's a distraction." Bear finished his coffee, set his cup down, and swung his arms out to the side and back again to stretch them out. "They could just be wasting our time. Having us look in one direction while they do something somewhere else."

"But why reach out at all?"

"What do you mean?"

Sadie settled further back into her chair. "They reached out to us first. We knew the agents were missing, but we didn't have any evidence as to where they went. The video was our first major clue. They had no reason to try to distract us."

"Rookie move?" Bear said.

"I guess." Sadie didn't sound convinced.

"Maybe they figured it was just a matter of time. That video was sent before the fire, which could mean they planted the body but didn't strike the match."

"That also means we have two players on the board unrelated to each other," Sadie said.

"Not unrelated," Bear said, "but definitely not working with each other. There's a reason why that Marine wanted to burn the place down that's related to the terrorists. We just have to figure out what that is."

Sadie made a note of something on her tablet. "The cell was definitely sending us a message. They wanted the body of that agent found. They wanted our attention, but I'm not convinced it's to get these guys out of jail."

"I might have gotten some good news in another department," Bear said.

Sadie's eyes lit up. "Jack?"

Bear nodded. "He was in London three weeks ago."

"What? Why? How do you know?"

"You're not the only one with contacts." Bear smiled, but it faded almost as soon as it formed. "And I don't know why he was here. He disappeared as soon as he landed. I'm still looking into it."

"Another dead end." Sadie held the paper cup to her chest like it was the only thing keeping her warm. "We keep hitting brick walls, Bear. I don't think we're meant to figure out what's going on here."

"There's one avenue we haven't fully explored yet," Bear said. "The kid."

"What about him?"

"Someone instructed him to pickpocket me. That means they knew I was here and they wanted to know why."

"The question is whether they're tied to the agents and the terrorist group or Jack."

"Or something else." When Sadie tilted her head to the side, Bear shrugged. "Given how this week is going, I wouldn't be surprised if the universe decided to throw something else at me."

"Keep your voice down, Bear." Sadie's voice was even, but she was smiling. "Don't anger the gods. We don't need that kind of trouble right now."

"We need to talk to Seamus again." Bear grabbed his jacket from the chair he'd tossed it on last night. "We need to find out who was behind his little scheme."

CHAPTER SIXTEEN

The first clue that something was off was the fact that they weren't greeted in the driveway when Sadie pulled up to the safe house. Bear leaned forward and noted all the lights were on, but there didn't seem to be a whole lot of movement inside. One of the cars was missing.

"What did I tell you about angering the gods?" Sadie said.

They stepped out of the car in unison, each one putting a hand on their weapon. Bear had a sinking feeling in his stomach. The safe house was secure. It was in a good location. But sometimes things went wrong. He hoped he wasn't about to find his worst nightmare inside.

Sadie led the way to the house, but as soon as they reached the steps, the door opened and Agent Bhandari filled the frame.

"Did HQ send you?" he asked.

"No," Bear said. "Why? What's going on?"

Bhandari ran a hand through his hair. There were several strands out of place, and Bear had a distinct feeling he'd been giving in to the nervous tic for a while now. "Seamus ran away."

"What?" Sadie's voice echoed around the entranceway. She took a step forward. "What happened?"

Bhandari put his hands up in surrender. "I don't know. I wasn't here. I left two of my agents to watch over him. They said he was sound asleep on the couch one minute and gone the next."

Bear muscled his way past Bhandari to check for himself. There was no Seamus in sight. And his shoes were gone too. "How long ago was this?"

"Couple hours," Bhandari said. "And before you shoot the messenger, Director Winters specifically told me to keep it quiet. My first suggestion was to bring you in, Mr. Logan, given your relationship with him."

"Lot of good that does us now." Bear tilted his head to the side, listening for any movement upstairs. "Where is everyone?"

"Scouting the neighborhood. He's gotta be out there somewhere. We're a ways from London. He wouldn't walk back all by himself."

"He's used to living on the streets," Bear said. "He's young and he's got a lot of energy. He's resourceful. He'd be able to do it."

Sadie paced along the center of the living room. "Run me through everything that happened since we were last here."

Bear could see the hesitation on Bhandari's face. "Winters doesn't need to know you told us," he said. "Let us help. We all want to find him, right? At the end of the day that's all she'll care about."

Bhandari rubbed a hand against the back of his neck, but Bear saw the moment he gave in to the logic.

"You left and we had him go through the Marines on the computer," Bhandari said. "Took a while. We had to do it in batches so he wouldn't get confused or too tired and miss something. On the fourth round of pictures, he pointed out the man he'd seen in the apartment."

"Who was it?" Sadie asked.

Bhandari grabbed the printouts from the table and leafed through a couple photos before pulling up the man's picture. "His name is Logan Miller. He has no record prior to enlisting in the Marines when he was eighteen. He's twenty-two now. He has an Other Than Honorable Conditions Discharge on his record. After that, he sort of fell off the map."

"Until he showed up in London and set fire to an apartment building," Bear asked. "What'd he do to get the discharge?"

"Excessive violence. He was a bit of a loose cannon. Drank a lot. He became a security threat." Bhandari traced his finger down the page and kept reading. "It says here he crossed the line on more than one occasion. Never did anything overt, but there were too many instances where his CO thought he was pushing his luck. Gave him a handful of warnings that Miller ignored. The CO decided to take action and he was discharged."

"Someone must've snatched him up," Bear said.

Sadie stopped pacing. "What do you mean?"

"I've seen guys like him before. Enlist at eighteen. Think they're gonna save the world. They like the action, the violence. They think they're hot shit and can get away with whatever they want. And when they get discharged, their life falls apart. They don't have anything else, so they do something drastic."

Sadie started pacing again. "Like what?"

"Like fall in with the wrong crowd," Bear said. "There are organizations out there that take advantage of guys like this. Someone like Miller wants that sense of family and purpose back. He was already used to stepping out of line, so doing something off the radar or straight up illegal doesn't really matter to him. Especially if it means he gets a slice of his old life back."

"You think he's working with someone else?" Bhandari asked.

"I think he's working *for* someone else," Bear said. "He's probably just a lackey. Hired to clean up a mess he had nothing to do with in the first place."

"But if we find Miller," Sadie said, "we'll find who he's working for."

"Exactly." Bear turned to Bhandari. "There's no other information in there about what he's been up to since he was discharged?"

Bhandari turned his attention back to the paper. "He went home to Georgia. Spent a couple months living with his mom, and then he just up and left. HQ is working on finding a paper trail, but if he's trying to keep a low profile, it'll likely be minimum."

"Georgia?" Sadie asked. She paused in her pacing and stared at Bear.

"That mean something to you?" he asked.

"He sounds like an all-American boy, doesn't he? Maybe someone who could have a hint of a Southern accent?"

"I feel like I'm missing something here," Bhandari said.

Bear didn't bother explaining. His mind was racing through the conversation they had with Maria. "We can't know for sure it's him. It could still be anyone."

"Could be, but what are the chances a Southern boy calls her up and gives her bad intel, and then another Southern boy turns up to clean up the mess that's left behind?"

"Not likely," Bear admitted. "You gotta find this guy."

"Me?" Sadie asked. "Where are you going?"

"Back to the apartment," Bear said. "I gotta find the kid."

"You think he's going back there?"

"I have no clue." Bear ran a hand down his beard. "But it's the last place he was before we transferred him here. He was hanging out there looking for me. Maybe he went back for some reason. Or maybe it's close enough to where he's used to hanging out that I'll find him eventually."

"That's a stretch, Bear," Sadie said. "He could be anywhere in London."

Bear shrugged. "Gotta start somewhere."

CHAPTER SEVENTEEN

Bear relegated himself to spending the night walking London's streets looking for a kid. He knew it was an impossible task, but he was tired of speculating about this or that. He needed to move. He needed action. He needed to get his hands dirty.

Right now, this was the closest he'd get to that. He leaned against the cold façade of a brick building, shrouded in shadows. The temperatures were likely below freezing, and the wind had whipped itself into a frenzy. He'd bought a scarf and a coffee to stay warm, but his fingers and ears were still suffering. It was going to be a long night if nothing happened.

He didn't have a plan other than keep his eyes peeled for Seamus. If he spotted him, what would he do? He could try to talk to him, ask him why he ran away. Or he could follow him and hope he'd be led back to his boss. Both scenarios were a needle-in-a-haystack proposal.

And there were other factors at play. He didn't know what Annie or their boss looked like, but it was clear both of them knew him. He'd have a hard time keeping a low profile. Suddenly his impossible task seemed like a complete waste of time.

But Bear didn't turn back. He finished his coffee, dumped the cup into a garbage can, and pulled his scarf up around his head, doing his best to hide as much of his face as possible. He shoved his hands deep into his pockets and started his trek toward the apartment building.

Bear had Sadie drop him off a couple blocks away before she returned to HQ to talk with Director Winters and help with the search for their Marine. The Director wasn't going to be happy that both of them had been brought into the loop thanks to Bhandari, but there also wasn't much she could do about it. They would've found out eventually. Bear figured Winters had wanted to find the kid and make sure he was okay before she troubled them with the news that he ran away.

But while the agents kept searching the residential area around the safe house, Bear made a beeline for Camden. Seamus had already been on his own for a couple of hours. If he was able to grab a train or a bus, it was likely he had already made it back to London.

Sadie was right, of course. Seamus could be anywhere, and as far as they knew, he had no reason to return to this area. But he also had a close relationship with Annie, who he'd been separated from for about a day now. They would've had a backup plan, or at least a meeting place, if something had gone wrong. It'd likely be close to where they had last seen each other, rather than somewhere across the city. This was the best starting point to look for the kid, even if everyone else thought he was crazy.

So he kept his head down and trudged on, following the circuit around the apartment building he had established when he was first staking it out. He wound his way closer and closer until he was on the same street. He could see the building in the distance. It was probably just his mind playing tricks on him, but he could swear he still smelled smoke in the air.

As he got closer, keeping to the shadows on the far side of the street, Bear noticed that the area around the building was void of any movement. It was like people thought it was cursed. By now reports would've come in about the mysterious dead body and the gas leak.

He wasn't sure how much Winters was able to keep out of the newspapers, but rumors spread, regardless. Even if the rumors were unsubstantiated, people let their imaginations run wild. And that always got the best of them.

Bear was just deciding whether he wanted to slip into an alley and keep an eye on the building or keep walking when a blur of color caught his attention. Bear knew immediately it was Seamus in those damn new shoes. The kid was running down the sidewalk, jumping from shadow to shadow, pausing every so often to make sure he wasn't being watched. Bear froze, but he wasn't too worried about being spotted. He was wearing all black and Seamus was in a rush.

"What are you doing, kid," Bear muttered to himself. He was worried. Seamus wasn't paying close enough attention, and his shoes practically lit up every time he ran through one of the pools of light from the street lamps.

But just like before, Seamus relied too much on his speed. He was clearly after something, and he thought that as long as he got to it quickly enough, he could escape without getting into too much trouble.

Bear held his breath as he watched Seamus veer off the sidewalk and into the grass in front of the apartment building. He looked around once, and then made his way over to the front steps. To the right was a small garden just beginning to turn green thanks to all the rain it'd been getting over the last couple days.

Seamus ignored the plants, and instead reached down to pick up a fist-sized rock. He tossed it to the side and started digging, tossing dirt behind him. After a few seconds he pulled something out of the ground and did a little fist pump. Bear would've thought it was comical if his some-bad-shit-is-about-to-go-down radar wasn't sounding the alert.

The kid pushed the dirt back in place to fill up the hole, replaced the rock, and stood up, staring down at whatever was in his hand. Then he placed it in his pocket and took off running. Without thinking, Bear stepped out of the shadows. He wasn't sure what he was planning on doing. It was much smarter to let Seamus run off and follow him, but Bear's instincts told him the kid wouldn't get far.

Seamus's attention snapped to Bear and his steps faltered. His eyes looked apologetic, but it was clear he wasn't going to stop and talk. Before Bear could call out to him, a white van tore around the corner and came barreling toward them.

Bear melted back into the shadows while Seamus froze. The men in the van didn't waste any time. They skidded to stop in front of Seamus, opened the side panel, and called out to him. Seamus took a step back, but it was too late. He should've already been running in the opposite direction. Should've ran toward Bear.

Two burly men jumped out of the van and grabbed Seamus by the arms. The kid screamed and kicked at them, but he was so tiny compared to the guys. There was no way he was going to escape their grip. And even if he did, each one had a rifle strapped to their back.

Bear's initial instinct was to throw caution to the wind and charge the van. But between the two men kidnapping Seamus and the two in the front of the vehicle, he was outnumbered and outgunned. So he stuck to the shadows. The smartest play was to wait and watch.

The man threw Seamus in the back, and the van took off before they even closed the side panel. It headed north.

Bear didn't waste any time. He sprinted up the street, found an older model sedan, and put his elbow through the window. No alarm sounded, and Bear quickly went to work hot-wiring the car. Seconds later, he was on the road and in pursuit of the van.

CHAPTER EIGHTEEN

Bear kept his distance but made sure he was never too far away from the van to risk losing track of Seamus and the men who took him. The broken window let in the cold April air, and if Bear wasn't already running on pure adrenaline, he'd have no trouble staying awake.

The guy driving the van kept to the speed limit and made sure to use his turn signals and brake well before any red lights or stop signs. Bear wasn't sure if it was because they suspected he was following them, or if it was because they knew if they got pulled over, they'd have an even bigger mess on their hands.

But they didn't have to worry about the cops. It didn't take long for the van to come to its final destination. They were in an industrial area, surrounded by warehouses and businesses like car repair shops and small factories.

A garage door opened and the van pulled inside. It was a narrow building only three stories high. The other buildings appeared to have been built in the last decade or so. This one seemed like it had been thrown up in the 1950s or earlier. Bear idly wondered if the other business owners thought of it as an eyesore or if it had particular historical value that made up for its ugliness.

He didn't waste much time trying to puzzle it out. Instead, he drove past the garage and parked in front of a metalworking shop just down the road. He turned off the car and stuck his hand out the window, manually tilting the side-view mirror up and out so he could keep an eye on the garage. It looked like a paint shop. Pretty convenient if you were in the business of kidnapping children. Changing vehicles quickly wouldn't be an issue at all.

The building was dark for only a couple minutes before a pair of lights lit up the top floor. A few shadows passed in front of the windows, but Bear had no way of telling how many people were inside or what the setup was like. The men in the van were heavily armed, so it stood to reason that their home base was, too.

Bear was still debating the best way to get into the building when a figure appeared out of a side door, pulled his hood up over his head, and looked up and down the street. Bear sunk down into his seat and waited. Apparently, there was nothing suspicious about the quiet street because he produced a key, locked the door, and took off in Bear's direction with his hands deep in his pockets.

Bear didn't waste time. As soon as the man was past him, he slipped out of the car, leaving the door slightly ajar so as to remain absolutely silent. He had always been light on his feet despite his size, and his time in the military only strengthened that particular talent. Used to drive Jack crazy. But it came in handy on more than one occasion.

Like this one.

The man didn't even realize what hit him before Bear's arms were around his neck, holding tight to cut off his air supply. The man tried to pull his handgun and aim it at Bear's face, but one sharp twist and a pop later, and the guy slumped in his arms. That would be one less person to deal with inside.

Bear dragged the man across the street and dumped him along the backseat of the car. It kind of looked like he was sleeping. And by the time anyone realized anything different, Bear would be long gone. Hopefully with Seamus in tow.

Once he secured the keys, Bear jogged back across the street and ran up to the door on the side of the building that led to the garage. He stood there for a moment and listened, but he couldn't hear any sounds from inside. The door was either too thick to let out any noise, or everyone was upstairs. He prayed it was the latter.

There were only a handful of keys on the keyring, and Bear got the right one on the second try. With one hand, he pulled his pistol from his waistband, and with the other, he slowly pushed the door open until he could take in the whole room.

Empty.

Or, at least, empty of people. The garage housed the van and one other car, a black and utterly average looking sedan they probably used when they needed a quick getaway car that would blend in with traffic. Whatever these guys were up to, they were smart enough to have a backup plan.

The room was also stacked with boxes and crates. As much as Bear wanted to know what was going on, he didn't think it was a good idea to take his time. He wasn't sure if the guys would kill Seamus, but he wasn't about to take that risk. The sooner he made his way up to the third floor, the better.

Bear crossed the room to the next door and pushed it open. The squeak of rusty hinges echoed up a narrow stairwell and he froze. The door was just wide enough for him to slip through without widening the gap any further, but when he let it fall shut behind him, he cringed as the hinges squeaked again in the other direction.

He waited at the base of the steps, listening to see if there was any movement above him. He couldn't even hear the men on the third floor, but at least they weren't rushing down the stairs to investigate the sound of the door opening.

After a minute of nothing but silence, he ascended the stairwell. He kept to the outside and pointed his pistol upward, making sure he'd get a shot off before anyone coming down after him even had time to find their mark. He only stopped moving once he reached the second landing.

Now he had a decision to make. He knew there were men on the third floor, but he couldn't guarantee there weren't some here either. He could clear the floor and risk wasting more time, or he could ambush the third-floor men and risk someone coming up behind him.

But if the men really wanted to kill Seamus and take whatever he had, they wouldn't have brought him back to the garage. They would've done the deed and dropped his body off in some alley. It was unlikely anyone would miss a homeless kid too much. And those who did weren't likely to go to the police to report him missing.

With his decision made, Bear twisted the handle on the second-floor door and thanked God these hinges weren't as rusty as the ones downstairs. Just like before, he slowly opened the door until he could see the whole room, and immediately patted himself on the back for having the sense to check this floor before he headed up to the next one.

Two men had their backs to the door. They were standing over a table with a desk lamp and some papers on it. The rest of the room was pretty bare, except for a few folding chairs and some more boxes and crates stacked in the corners.

As much as he was curious about the contents of those packages, he needed to neutralize these two before he went upstairs. The only problem was he couldn't risk either one of them firing a weapon and alerting anyone upstairs.

Bear made a snap decision. He kept low and rushed at the men, using the butt of his sidearm to knock one unconscious before the other even noticed. When the second man, who had fiery red hair and a splash of freckles across his face, realized what was happening, he reached for a pistol sitting on the table.

But Bear was faster. He kicked at the man's knee and sent him to the ground, the pistol spinning away across the floor, well out of reach. Freckles tried to reach up and put his hands around Bear's neck, but his grip was weak. Bear broke the hold and punched him in the gut to steal his breath away. As the man was gasping, Bear delivered a strike to knock him out.

Knowing he only had a minute or two before they woke up, Bear found some rope and tied them back to back. A roll of duct tape sat on the table. He used that to silence both of them.

He circled the room once to make sure there wasn't anyone else hiding in the shadows, and then went back to the table in the center of the room. He adjusted the light closer so he could see the plans in front of him. They looked like schematics for a tunnel or subway system.

The first man started to wake up, but Bear didn't cast him more than a cursory glance to make sure his bonds were still tight before returning his attention to the problem at hand. He ruffled through the papers, but it didn't seem like they were planning to bomb anything. It was just different views of what looked like an abandoned tunnel, plus some potential routes to get in and out of it.

Bear grabbed a crowbar from nearby and pried open the top of the nearest crate. Inside were dozens of tiny replicas of the iconic red telephone box you saw everywhere in souvenir shops around London. It didn't take a genius to figure out what they were for, and sure enough, when Bear slid open a false bottom, several tiny bags of cocaine spilled out.

Turns out he had stumbled onto a drug trafficking operation by accident.

Apparently, it was just going to be one of those days. First it was Jack. Then a mystery Marine and a homeless kid, followed by terrorists. Now he had to deal with a gang of drug traffickers too. He was getting too goddamn old for all this excitement.

Bear double-checked the ropes that kept the two men in place. They were both awake now, but they weren't going anywhere. Freckles still looked a little groggy, but the first man was glowering at Bear *hard*.

"Sorry, boys," Bear said. "Gotta go pay your friends a visit now."

Without waiting for a muffled response, Bear made his way back to the stairwell and up to the third floor. From this vantage point, he could hear someone talking on the other side of the door, but he couldn't make out any of the words.

Chances are there were still a couple of guys inside, and with the kid in there, Bear didn't want to go charging in and risk injuring him. Or worse. But someone was bound to wonder what was taking the guy in the hoodie so long to get back, or even why the two men on the second floor hadn't returned.

So Bear decided to watch and wait.

CHAPTER NINETEEN

Bear had crept back down to the second floor and slipped back inside the room. He knelt down next to the wall, keeping the door slightly ajar so he could hear if someone was coming. He hoped it would be someone from the third floor and not anyone new entering via the garage, but he had a good vantage point for both directions.

Sure enough, after about fifteen or twenty minutes, Bear heard the door upstairs open. Laughter filled the stairwell before it was once again muffled as the door swung shut. Heavy footsteps pounded down the stairs, but it only sounded like there was one of them.

"Yo, Patrick," the man called out as he reached the second-floor landing. "Boss man says gets your ass—"

His words were cut off as he opened the door and noticed the two other men struggling against the ropes. Bear tackled the newcomer to the floor. He put one hand over his mouth, while he held the pistol to his head.

"Shit," Bear said, finally taking a good look at the man he had pinned. His hair was cropped short and the whiskers on his chin were thin and patchy, but it was clear he was a natural-born redhead. He looked a little like Freckles, and Bear wondered if maybe they were related. Either way, he couldn't be any older than eighteen. "What're you doing mixed up in all of this, kid?"

Whiskers tried to respond, but Bear didn't lift his hand. Or move his gun, despite the tears in the kid's eyes. He deserved to be scared straight. Before something worse happened.

"This is what's going to happen," Bear said. "I'm going to move my hand and let you up. You're going to sit yourself down in one of those very nice folding chairs and keep your eyes shut until I tell you otherwise, you got me?"

The kid nodded his head as vigorously as he could under the pressure of Bear's hand.

When Bear lifted his hand, Whiskers didn't make a sound. Bear removed his weight and let the kid stand up. Shaking and openly crying now, Whiskers walked to the other side of the room, casting a glance every few seconds at the other men tied to the chair.

Bear waited until the kid sat down and squeezed his eyes shut before he found another length of rope and tied him to the chair. He tore off a piece of duct tape, but didn't stick it to his mouth just yet.

"You can open your eyes," Bear said.

Whiskers followed his instructions.

"How many people are upstairs?" Bear asked.

Whiskers glanced at the two men next to him. When he looked back at Bear, he shook his head.

"Look, you're fucked either way," Bear said. He purposely gestured with the hand that held the gun. He didn't miss the way Whiskers followed his every movement. "Right now, your best bet is to tell me what I need to know. Once my business is finished upstairs, I'm gonna call the cops and you're all going to jail. You will be tied to this chair when they arrive. The difference is whether they'll find you alive or not."

Whiskers shuddered. "Three. Three people."

"Including the kid?"

Whiskers nodded.

"What's the layout of the room?"

"One big room, plus a bathroom off to the right." He cleared his throat. "There's a-a couch in the middle. And a couple chairs, a TV."

"They got guns up there?"

Whiskers nodded.

"Any other surprises I need to know about?" Bear asked.

"They've been drinking," he answered.

"You did good." Bear placed the strip of duct tape across the kid's mouth. "Let this be a lesson for you. Don't make the same mistake twice."

Bear turned to Freckles and the other guy. "And you two assholes should know better than to bring a kid into an operation like this. He was gonna get shot sooner rather than later and that would've been on you."

Freckles looked angry, but Bear could see the fear in his eyes. The other guy just kept trying to struggle out of his ropes. Bear wasn't worried. The cops would be here before any of them had a chance of slipping free.

Bear didn't waste any time making his way back to the third floor. He kept his pistol aimed forward and opened the door like they were expecting him. Any hesitation would've tipped them off, and the few seconds it would take for the men inside to register he wasn't one of theirs would be enough for him to get the drop on them.

He was already three steps into the room before the first man realized what was going on. He had hair so blond it was practically white, and he wore a newsboy cap to top it all off. The other man had been lounging on the couch, his feet up on the armrest. He didn't even bother looking up until Newsboy shouted.

"Who the fuck are you?"

Bear didn't bother answering. Instead, he struck out at the man's gut, knocking the air from him before throwing an uppercut and breaking his nose. Blood streamed from Newsboy's face, but it didn't slow him down. He charged at Bear just as the other man, who was inexplicably dressed in suspenders, jumped to his feet and pointed a gun in their direction.

Bear ducked and grabbed Newsboy's waist, spinning the pair of them. When Suspenders' shot rang out, it hit Newsboy in the shoulder and made him cry out in pain. Bear took advantage of their momentary shock by aiming his pistol and putting a bullet between Suspenders' eyes. He slumped back down to the couch.

Newsboy recovered and tried to swing at Bear, but in a daze of pain and confusion, he missed. Bear aimed at the man's knee cap and squeezed the trigger once. Newsboy collapsed to the floor in agony.

Bear's frantic eyes searched the room and found Seamus huddling against the wall. He was silent, but there were tears streaming down his face.

"You okay, kid?" Bear asked. He wanted to give Seamus his full attention, but he had to clear the bathroom first. If Whiskers was lying about how many people were in the room, they could both end up dead. "Did they hurt you?"

When he was sure the bathroom was empty, Bear turned back to Seamus, who hadn't moved. Bear took a deep breath and tried to regulate the adrenaline pumping through his system. He tucked his sidearm away and held up his hands.

"I'm not going to hurt you, Seamus," he said. "I just want to make sure you're okay."

Seamus nodded and wiped the tears from his eyes.

"Did they hurt you?" When Seamus shook his head, Bear asked, "Why'd you run away, buddy? I thought we had a deal."

Seamus remained silent and Bear could tell he wasn't going to spill his secrets just yet. Instead, Bear turned back to Newsboy. He knelt down next to the man and snapped a finger in front of his face to get his attention. He looked pale, but he was in no danger of bleeding out.

"What's your name?" Bear asked.

"Go to hell," the man spat.

Bear sighed. "Look, I've had a long day. I got three of your buddies tied up downstairs, and I already had to kill two others, including your friend over there. I'm not really in the mood for this whole back and forth bullshit."

Newsboy's gaze flickered to the sofa and back. He gritted his teeth. "James."

"Great. James. I'm sorry I shot you in the knee, but you were kind of pissing me off." Bear wiped the sweat off his brow. "I'd really rather not kill you, and I really don't want to put a bullet in your other kneecap. I just have one question, and if you answer me directly, you're gonna go to jail instead of a grave. That sound good?"

James looked like it pained him in more than one way, but he nodded.

"Good." Bear hooked a thumb over his shoulder. "Why'd you kidnap the kid?"

"He had something we needed," James answered.

"What was it?"

"I don't know."

Bear stood up and racked the handgun's slide. A round popped out and landed on the guy's chest as a fresh bullet chambered. "I thought we had an agreement, James."

James looked panicked. He tried to shift away. "I don't know. Honest. It was some sort of file the boss was looking at. It's on his computer over there."

Bear turned to face the couch and noticed a laptop on the coffee table. Sure enough, there was a flash drive sticking out of the side, and a bunch of blueprints were pulled up on the screen. Bear grabbed it and held it in front of James' face.

"What is this?"

James gazed at the screen. "It-it looks like plans for the tunnel we were gonna use for our next op. But it's all wrong."

"What do you mean it's all wrong?"

James pointed at the screen. "I don't know what these symbols are. This isn't our schematic. Not unless the boss changed it on us."

Bear flipped the computer back around and looked closely at the screen. It only took him a minute to put this part of the puzzle together. And suddenly a few of the disjointed pieces that had been trailing him since he'd landed in London started coming together.

He'd stumbled onto some sort of drug trafficking ring, but it looked like these guys had unknowingly uncovered someone else's plans to blow up the same tunnel they were going to use. Seamus had retrieved the flash drive from the apartment the agents had been hiding out in, which meant there was a pretty big chance this belonged to the terrorist organization who had executed one of Sadie's men.

The question now was why Seamus was involved in all of this. He wasn't working for the gang, that was obvious. Was he or his boss working for the terrorists? If so, how the hell did a twelve-year-old kid get wrapped up in all of that?

But when Bear turned around to ask Seamus just that, he stopped dead.

The kid was gone. He'd slipped out from underneath Bear's nose for a second time.

CHAPTER TWENTY

Bear sat at the bar at Cataldi's nursing his third beer. He hadn't seen the woman from last time, but the man who'd served him before was currently wiping down the counter and checking that his other patrons didn't need anything. All in all, it was a pretty quiet evening.

Bear had called the cops the second he'd vacated the building, even telling them about the guy in the car. He was sure his finger-prints were all over that car and the dead body, but he wasn't too worried about it. Sadie would find a way to cover it all up. And if she didn't, it wouldn't be too much trouble to tell them at least part of the story. He was trying to help Seamus. He was attacked. He was defending his life.

Once he was clear of the crime scene, Bear had taken his time getting to the restaurant. A cab brought him most of the way, but he got out several blocks over and meandered his way through the streets. He knew he was being watched and he wanted to be seen. The whole point was to go back to the beginning, to where this mess had started in the first place.

It was just as Bear drained the last drops of his beer that a man sat down next to him. Bear could've called Sadie and set up another meeting, but he was testing a theory. Even after their business was done, Mr. Jones was keeping an eye on the situation.

The question was, who was he keeping an eye on the situation for?

"Hello." Bear didn't even bother turning in his chair.

"Good evening, Mr. Logan." His accent was just as thick as Bear remembered, with that hint of something from Eastern Europe.

"How did you know I was looking for you?"

Mr. Jones ordered them a pair of beers. "I had a hunch."

"You don't seem like the kind of guy who usually relies on hunches."

"And you don't seem like the kind of guy who leaves something to chance."

Bear took a swig of his beer. "Guess we're both acting out of character tonight."

Mr. Jones chuckled. "What is it you want, Mr. Logan?"

"Why have you been watching me?" Bear asked. "Is that what the extra money was for?"

Mr. Jones' face was the epitome of innocence. "Extra money?"

"An address shouldn't have cost as much as I gave you," Bear said.

"Depends on how difficult it was to get."

"True." Bear wiped the condensation off the bottle in his hands. "But you seem like a resourceful guy. I don't think it was too difficult for you."

"You flatter me."

Bear took that as confirmation. "How do you typically get your information?"

"A good magician never reveals his secrets."

"I'm assuming your network is pretty large. You've worked with our mutual friend in the past, so I'm also assuming you come across highly valuable intel." Bear was tired of the back and forth. It was time to go big or go home. "No offense, but you don't scream government agent to me. Which means you need to get your information the old-fashioned way."

"And what way is that, Mr. Logan?"

"With a little bit of money invested, you can build a team of trusted individuals. People who do all your legwork. People on the streets."

"You mean the homeless?" Mr. Jones asked.

Bear shrugged. "The homeless. And Taxi drivers. Waiters. Drug dealers. Anyone who would be underappreciated and overlooked."

"You're beating around the bush a little bit too much for my tastes, Mr. Logan. What is it you're asking me?"

"Have you been watching me since I landed?"

"You already know the answer to that question, but for the sake of our relationship, I will choose to be direct with you. Yes, I have."

"Direct." Bear scoffed. That was a first. "Did our mutual friend hire you to do so?"

"Yes, she did." Mr. Jones paused. "She warned me you liked to get into trouble. I was to ensure your safety. If anyone reached out to you, I was to report back. If I noticed something you didn't, I was to report back. You get the idea."

Bear wasn't sure if he was grateful Sadie was just trying to look out for him, or if he was bothered by the fact that she was keeping secrets. He appreciated the gesture, but now it just felt like he was wasting time talking to Mr. Jones when he could be elsewhere.

"Is the kid yours?"

"I beg your pardon?" Mr. Jones asked.

"The kid," Bear said. "Seamus. Is he one of yours?"

"He is."

Bear could feel the heat rising in his cheeks. It didn't help that it was fueled by alcohol. "Do you often put kids in dangerous situations like that?"

"I prefer not to." Mr. Jones had the decency to look somber. "It is never my intention."

"It's your intention if there's even a remote possibility of something like that happening." Bear noticed one or two other patrons looking in his direction and worked to control his voice. "Seamus could've been killed tonight. It seems like you're not hurting for money. Why don't you use those funds to keep kids off the street instead?"

Mr. Jones' face flushed, but his tone implied it was with anger, not shame. "What I do with my money is my business, Mr. Logan. But to ensure that we're perfectly clear, I will say this. I do what I can to keep all of my informants safe. I take no pleasure in using children to gather information. Seamus's job was to watch both the building and you from a distance. It seems he wanted to impress a young girl and decided to take an unnecessary risk. And, as I remember and feel compelled to point out, you're the one who sent him into a building without knowing who or what was inside."

Bear gritted his teeth, but he couldn't argue. They both hadn't done the most they could for Seamus. The fire inside of him died down to a dull roar.

"But that's not entirely true, is it?"

"Come again?"

Bear took a sip of his beer so he could choose his words carefully. "Seamus told me he was instructed to take both my wallet and my phone. Why are you lying to me, Jones?"

"Mr. Jones," he corrected. "And I suppose old habits die hard."

"Why did you want my phone?"

"Information." Mr. Jones gestured at the world around him. "It's why I do everything I do."

"Our contact told you to watch me, but didn't tell you why?"

"She knows how to compartmentalize information. I didn't need to know what was going on in order to keep an eye on you."

"But you wanted it anyway."

Mr. Jones shrugged, a soft smile playing around his lips. "I'm an inherently greedy person. I have grown to accept that about myself."

"Is Seamus okay?"

"He is," Mr. Jones replied. "A little shaken up, but his friend Annie is taking care of him."

"You're the boss he's not allowed to meet."

A sad smile formed on Mr. Jones' face. "It's better for the kids not to know who I am. It keeps them safer."

"He's a good kid," Bear said. "He deserves better than this."

"I know." Mr. Jones pushed his still-full beer a little farther from him. "We're working on it. For him and Annie, too. For all the kids who don't have parents or a bed to sleep in. We do what we can, I promise you that."

Bear didn't bother asking who *we* was. He knew he wasn't going to get that answer out of his mysterious contact. But he did have one other pressing question. "How did Seamus know to look for the flash drive?"

Mr. Jones turned his whole body to look at Bear. "What flash drive?"

Bear laughed. "You don't need to pretend like you don't know. I'm sure Seamus told Annie everything the moment he was reunited with her, and she filled you in on everything he said. In fact, I'm guessing the only real reason why you're here right now is because you want information only I have."

Mr. Jones smiled, and Bear could see the calculation in his eyes. "He mentioned the flash drive. He said he saw one of the agents bury it about a week ago. Right before they went missing."

"You knew about this and didn't go after it yourself?"

"It was tempting," Mr. Jones said. "But I'm more interested in who else wants to know what's on that flash drive. That seems like the more valuable information to me."

"So why did Seamus grab it now?"

"It had been over a week. One agent was dead. I figured I'd get my hands on it before you did. The universe had other plans, I suppose."

Bear chugged the rest of his beer and dropped a couple bills on the table. "I tell you this, and you back off. You keep your distance and let me do my thing. And the kid stays far away from this."

Mr. Jones didn't even hesitate. "Done."

"I don't know who they are, but they seemed like an Irish gang. Maybe a family business. They wanted to use an abandoned tunnel to transport drugs. My guess is they were also watching the apartment building. They knew the information was there, but they didn't know where. Figured someone would retrieve it eventually. When Seamus dug it up, they were ready."

"He's lucky you were there, Mr. Logan."

"Yeah." Bear pushed his stool back up against the bar. "Make sure he stays lucky."

"I'll honor our deal," Mr. Jones said. "You have my word."

CHAPTER TWENTY-ONE

Bear left the restaurant without a backwards glance at Mr. Jones. He doubted the guy would be able to resist keeping an eye on Bear entirely, but as long as he stayed out of the way, Bear didn't care. There were too many unknown factors, and he was getting tired of chasing ghosts. He had to eliminate what he could and focus on anything that remained.

Which meant the next obvious step was to talk to Sadie.

Bear found a bench down the street and took out his phone. His finger hovered over the send button. He didn't like the hesitation he was feeling. He didn't like that he wasn't sure he could trust her.

Jack and Bear hadn't known Sadie for long, but Costa Rica had bonded the three of them in a way that only happened during harrowing experiences. Korea had complicated that relationship, but Bear had decided to trust her. She had used him to get to Thorne, but Bear couldn't say he wouldn't have done the same in that situation. And he wasn't exactly upset at the result.

So why was he having trouble trusting her now? She had paid Mr. Jones to keep an eye on him. Was she worried about his safety, or was she worried he was going to keep something from her? Was there something she was afraid he'd find out? Something more she was hiding from him?

Could it have to do with the agents? They had been her men, after all. And Bear was fairly certain one of them was dirty. Why else would he be burying flash drives in the front yard of an apartment complex? Maybe Sadie wanted to keep that quiet so her superiors didn't have another reason to pull her from the field. Or maybe she wasn't as clean as he wanted her to be, either.

Or did all of this secrecy have something to do with Jack? She had seemed pretty surprised when Bear had informed her Jack had been in London. Was that because she hadn't expected him to be so close, or was it because she thought he was somewhere else?

It took all of Bear's willpower not to chuck his phone against the nearest building and walk away from this entire mess. He could drop the gang, the terrorists, even the agents and Sadie without losing any sleep at night. The CIA and MI5 had enough resources to get the job done without him.

But he couldn't walk away from Jack.

Bear took a deep breath. One step at a time. Eliminate what he could. Focus on what remained.

Sadie picked up on the second ring. "Got anything for me?"

Bear ignored the question. "What'd you find out about our Marine?"

Sadie took a deep breath. "Not as much as I was hoping, but we've got some promising leads. He stayed off the radar for a couple years after he was discharged, but in the last year or so we've found him popping up here and there under other names."

"How'd you find him?"

"They've got some pretty good people here at MI5, but don't tell them I said that." She laughed but Bear had no urge to join in. "We were able to track down a few of his friends from his military days and worked out from there. He visited one or two of them a couple times. The trail was faint, but we were able to follow it. We're getting a better sense of who this guy is."

"And who's that?"

Sadie blew out a breath and it crackled in Bear's ear. "You were right about his life after getting discharged. Looks like he does cleanup jobs here and there. Nothing solid that we can link him to, but it at least tells us what to watch for."

"And that would fall in line with what he was doing at the apartment," Bear said. "If he's a cleaner now, his job would've been to recover any evidence from the scene and then destroy everything else."

"But he wanted to burn the place down. That's less of a cleanup and more of a demolition."

Bear shrugged even though Sadie couldn't see it. "Whoever he's working for knew we were going to look in on the agents eventually. Slowing us down was probably the smartest option."

"But you got a drop on him." Sadie sounded proud. "It didn't quite pan out the way they wanted it to."

"True, but we're still twiddling our thumbs over here."

"Not necessarily." Sadie paused, and Bear had a feeling it was for dramatic effect. "We found our Marine leaving London hours after the fire. He made a single phone call from a pay phone prior to that. We're still tracking that information, but I've got a good feeling about this, Bear."

"You think it'll lead us to where he is?"

"That, and maybe who he's working for, too." When Bear didn't share in her excitement, she asked, "Is everything okay?"

"Yeah." Bear decided to keep the information about Mr. Jones to himself for now, but he had to share news about Seamus. "Yeah, just a lot going on all at once. I found the kid, though."

"You did?" Her voice was shrill. "Is he okay?"

"He's fine. A little shaken up. We kind of got ambushed."

"What happened?" Sadie's voice dropped to a deadly octave. "Are you hurt?"

"I'm fine. We're both fine. Everything is okay." Bear took a deep breath before launching into his story. "Bottom line is I found him back near the apartment. He dug up a flash drive in the front yard and then was immediately kidnapped. I think it was an Irish gang, but I don't have any clue who they are."

"Were you able to follow them?" she asked.

"Sure did. In fact, a few of them are still tied up, waiting for someone to arrest their asses. I'll send you the address. I don't know how much this ties into your agents. Probably best to at least poke around."

"And Seamus?"

Bear hesitated. He couldn't exactly tell her Seamus disappeared but that he knew he was okay. That information had come from Mr. Jones. "He's good. His friend Annie picked him up. They're both safe and they're going to lay low."

"Bear—"

"I don't like it any more than you do," he said. "But it's the best I could do in the moment. Besides, we have a bigger problem."

"The flash drive?"

"Yep." Bear patted his pocket to reassure himself it was still in there. "It looks like the Irish gang wanted to use some abandoned tunnel to house and transport their drugs, but there was a little bit of territory dispute."

"With who?" she asked.

"Our favorite group of unidentified terrorists. Turns out this flash drive belonged to them. They have plans to blow the tunnel to kingdom come."

Sadie was silent for a minute. "But why would the flash drive be buried in the front yard of the apartment building? They wouldn't have planted it there, which means—"

Bear was just about to confirm her greatest fear, that one or more of her men might've been working for the other side, when a thin wire passed down in front of his eyes and tightened around his throat. Bear dropped his phone and scrambled to pull at the garrote, but it was already cutting into his neck, slicing at his skin until he started bleeding.

Bear was used to fighting for his life, but usually he saw death coming at him head first. This time, he barely had time to assess the situation before his air supply started to run out.

CHAPTER TWENTY-TWO

As the wire sunk deeper into his neck, Bear knew he only had one option: stop struggling. His body screamed to fight back, but he knew it would just make the situation worse. With the garrote tight around his throat, Bear had to find a way to loosen it without causing more damage.

Instead of pulling away, Bear pressed himself against the back of the bench. He brought up first one foot, and then the other. He pushed with all his strength, forcing himself backwards over the bench. He collapsed on top of the person behind him and immediately the garrote loosened around his neck. Bear didn't waste his opportunity.

Bear flipped over and pinned the man who had nearly killed him. He had dark golden skin, a clean-shaven face, and wore dark clothes, black gloves, and a hat that barely covered his brown hair.

Bear took this all in within seconds, delivering several punches to the guy's face. There was a grunt, then an exhalation of air. The man was out for now, but it wouldn't last long.

Feeling that his eyes were wild as he looked up, Bear took in his surroundings. Four other figures emerged from the shadows, all dressed similarly to the first man. Each one of them had Middle-Eastern features, wore black street clothes, and had on gloves and a cap. Three of them wielded knives, while the fourth had a garrote just like the first man.

Bear knew they meant business, and weren't amateurs, when all four of them attacked at once. He barely had enough time to react before they were on him, but the bench that had nearly been his undoing a few seconds earlier was now his salvation.

Hopping to the other side, Bear kept it between him and the four attacking men. It forced them to split up into pairs and circle around, but it bought Bear just enough time to get his bearings and formulate a plan. It was a pretty basic plan, but a plan nonetheless.

Don't die.

Jack would've appreciated the simplicity of it, and for a moment, Bear wanted more than anything to see his friend materialize out of the darkness to stand at his side. Jack loved a good fight, and even though he was a crazy son of a bitch, he had a habit of winning them.

Bear hoped his own luck wasn't about to run out.

The pair on the left moved first, so Bear took them head on. He jabbed one in the neck and followed it up with a strike to the guy's nose, leaving him unable to breathe and see. His partner swung wide, attempting to take Bear out. He blocked the attack. The first man recovered more quickly than Bear anticipated and his knife found Bear's arm.

With a grunt, Bear pushed back at the second man's elbow and snapped his arm. There was a scream, but Bear cut it off with a jab to the throat that left the guy gagging for air. Bear turned his attention back to the man who'd stabbed him and didn't waste any time. A Spartan kick to the chest was enough to knock him down and give Bear the room he needed to turn his attention back to the second pair of men, who were creeping up behind him.

Bear grabbed for the man with the garrote, who made excellent armor against the other one with the knife. A perfect blow to the chest meant Bear felt the life slip away from his human shield, but it also took one more person out of the equation.

Removing his weapon from the chest of his friend, the man swung at Bear and caught him across the chest. Another slice of pain sharpened Bear's vision. It was like everything slowed down to a snail's pace. He could see the trajectory of the man's next move like there was a neon sign with a step-by-step guide.

Bear ducked the attack and tackled the man, throwing him against the edge of the bench. There was a loud pop and a howl of pain. The force had been enough to break something, but Bear wasn't in the mood to take chances. He wrested the knife from the man's hand and buried it to the hilt in the side of his neck.

That was another one down.

As Bear crawled off the second dead man, someone sliced at his arm again, cutting across the wound that was already there. An involuntary scream left his lips, but he didn't wait to register the full extent of the pain. Instead, he turned to find the man he'd Spartan kicked was back for more.

Bear was only too happy to oblige.

Without a weapon, he had to dodge the other man's harried attempts to slice and dice him. But it only took one wrong move to give Bear the opening he needed. Off balance from a missed slash, the man couldn't jump back quickly enough to stop Bear from grabbing his wrist and wrested the knife from him. A stab to the gut, the chest, and finally through the center of his neck was enough to make the third man fall.

Two more to go.

The one with the broken arm had switched his weapon to his other hand. He was less of a threat now that his dominant arm was out of commission, but Bear could also see the first man, the one who'd tried to get a jump on him with the garrote, rising from the pavement, his face a bloody mess.

Bear ignored the pain in his arm and his chest and chose to go for the easy shot. He struck out with his fist, connecting with the man's broken elbow. That's all it took to bring him to his knees, where Bear took his neck and snapped it. The man slumped to the ground.

"You don't have to die like your friends," Bear said, turning to the final man. He picked up the remaining knife and held it with a reverse grip, the blade out toward his enemy. "We can talk this out."

The remaining man didn't bother answering. He rounded the bench, garrote in hand, keeping his center of gravity low. His face was still bleeding, but his eyes were wide. The injuries were superficial, which meant he was automatically better off than Bear.

Instead of waiting to be on the defensive, Bear attacked. He launched forward and swiped for the man's neck. But his opponent was quick, using Bear's momentum to knock him sideways and off-balance. While Bear righted himself, the other man wrapped the wire around his neck again, fitting it along the bloody line it had already carved earlier in the fight.

It wasn't ideal, but at least the man was closer now. Bear twisted around, ignoring the searing pain across his neck, and drove the knife into his opponent's side. He could feel it meeting flesh and bone, but the other man didn't loosen his grip.

Bear pulled the knife free and drove it forward again. But instead of jumping away, the man just leaned back and pulled on the wire even harder. With it digging into his skin and cutting off his air, Bear made one final attempt. He freed the knife and then drove it up into the man's armpit.

It was enough to loosen the garrote. Bear pulled free of the weapon, twisted around, and drove the knife into the man's chest for the final time. That kept him down for good.

Five to zero. Bear's favor.

CHAPTER TWENTY-THREE

Bear was in a daze when the cops arrived. Sadie showed up within a few minutes and deescalated the entire situation. He didn't bother listening. The pain in his shoulder and chest filled his mind. It was easier if he didn't move. Easier if he concentrated on the mechanics of the fight rather than the results.

Before he knew it, Bear was sitting in the back of an ambulance while someone checked him out. Sadie was staring at him, disbelief in her eyes.

"What?" he asked. It sounded like his voice was at the end of a tunnel.

"What do you mean *what*? Bear, do you know what you look like right now?"

Bear looked down at his chest. He was covered in blood and he was pretty sure most of it wasn't his. His face felt raw and his knuckles were bruised. "Like shit?"

She laughed. "Yeah, like shit. You're gonna need stitches."

"No hospitals."

Sadie said, "Bear, those cuts on your arm are deep. You need stitches. Probably antibiotics to stave off infection."

Bear shook his head but didn't verbally argue. He knew he'd be in bigger trouble if he didn't get fixed up before going back into the fray.

"I'll meet you there, okay?" Sadie said. She looked back at the bloody scene behind them and then returned her gaze to Bear. "Let me just make sure we're wrapped up here, and then we'll talk, okay?"

Bear nodded and allowed himself to be placed on a stretcher. Sadie walked away, casting a furtive glance over her shoulder, while Bear was lifted into the ambulance and taken to the hospital at top speed.

The rest was a blur. He remembered arriving in the emergency room, assuring everyone that it looked worse than it felt. Still, he didn't say no to the pain meds they put him on. It made his whole body feel like it had been submerged in a warm bath.

There were no broken bones and no concussion. A cute nurse with her wavy hair in a ponytail told jokes while she stitched him up. He chuckled in all the right parts, and when she left, he settled back with a smile on his face.

But it was short lived.

Sadie popped in twenty minutes later, looking relieved. "It's nice to see you're no longer covered in blood."

Bear made a noncommittal sound and Sadie frowned.

"You've been acting weird since earlier tonight." She pulled the singular chair closer to his bed and sat down. "What's wrong? Did something else happen?"

Maybe it was the pain medication or maybe Bear was just tired of not getting direct answers. Either way, he decided he was done playing games. "You hired Mr. Jones to follow me."

Sadie froze, and then closed her eyes and pinched the bridge of her nose. "You weren't supposed to find out about that."

"Clearly."

"It's not what you think."

"And what do I think it is?"

"Look, Bear, I know how you feel. I know what this job does to us. The constant paranoia. I know you count the number of people you trust on one hand, and at the end of the day the only person you've ever been able to really rely on is Jack. I know this probably made you question a lot of our interactions, especially given what happened in Korea."

She wasn't wrong, but Bear wasn't going to admit that.

"I'm just worried," Sadie said. "About you and Jack. I feel like something else is going on here. Something behind the scenes that neither one of us can see. Mr. Jones is a good contact. He knows almost everything that goes on in London."

"Does he know about Jack?" Bear asked.

She smiled but it was filled with sadness. "I said *almost* everything."

"Figures."

"I didn't want to tell you because I knew you wouldn't appreciate me worrying about you. And I thought it would be best if no one else knew about Mr. Jones' involvement except for me."

"Because—"

"No." Sadie's voice was firm. "Before you say it, the answer is no."

Bear threw up his one good arm. "You don't even know what I was going to say."

"You were going to say, *because you don't trust me to keep my mouth shut* or something like that."

"I do not sound like that," Bear said. "I'm offended."

"Am I right?" she asked.

Bear tried to lie, but he couldn't grasp the right words.

"Exactly," Sadie said. She had a smug smile on her face, but she sobered quickly. "It had nothing to do with how much I trust you. I had a feeling this would all go to shit, and I needed someone on the outside to keep me informed. The fewer people who knew about it, the better. I was just trying to keep you safe."

"I don't appreciate the methods," Bear said. "But I appreciate the gesture."

"Noted." Sadie looked like she was searching for the right words before finally landing on, "I'm sorry."

"But this is about more than just keeping me safe," Bear said. "It's also about Jack."

Sadie opened her mouth to argue, but closed it and nodded. A slight blush crept into her cheeks.

"What's going on between you two?" Bear grunted as he shifted in his bed. "I mean, really?"

"Nothing." When Bear looked skeptical, Sadie became insistent. "Really. Nothing. I care about him. I think he cares about me, too..."

"He does."

She raised an eyebrow, but kept going. "But nothing is going on between us. I don't even think I want there to be anything between us. Jack is—"

"A pain in the ass?"

"Complicated," Sadie said, but she was smiling. "And I don't need more complications in my life."

"So, after this?" Bear asked. He had trouble saying it, trouble believing it, but he forced the words out anyway. "After we find him?"

Sadie threw back her head and laughed. "Oh, you're not getting rid of me that easily."

"Good." Bear met her eyes when he said it. "You're turning out to be almost as big of a pain in the ass as Jack. Maybe that's why I like you."

Sadie's face fell. "I owe you guys a lot after Costa Rica."

"Stop. Don't start that."

"But," Sadie continued, giving Bear a stern look, "it's more than that. If there were more people like you two in the world, it would be a better place."

"I'm not so sure about that. But I'll take the compliment." He glanced down at himself. "Might be the only way I can get you to leave me alone so I can enjoy what's left of the buzz from the pain meds."

Sadie cleared her throat and pulled her phone out of her pocket. "Fat chance. Maybe then we can get down to business?"

"Thank Christ," Bear said, but he was grateful for their heart-to-heart. "What've you got?"

"We think we've got some information on the terrorists."

"You think?" Bear asked.

Sadie gave him a half-hearted shrug. "Kind of hard to know. They're basically neo jihadists. It's a new faction that's popped up in London whose ideals are more aggressive and forward thinking than traditional jihadist motivations."

"More aggressive?" Bear had first-hand experience with these guys. "Is that possible?"

"Oh, it's possible." Sadie swiped through some screens on her phone. "They're less concerned about spreading their political agenda and more interested in watching the world burn. We're talking about major targeted violence with the most destruction possible."

"Which explains the plans for the tunnel," Bear said.

"Do you have the flash drive still?"

Bear reached for his shirt and pulled the drive from his pocket and handed it over. "It's all yours."

Sadie tucked it away. "I'll hand this off to Director Winters. They should be able to locate the tunnel based off the blueprints and make sure it's under lock and key moving forward."

Sadie's phone buzzed in her hand. "Speak of the devil," she said before answering. "Hello?"

Bear watched as Sadie's face went from passive to excited to determined. She put one hand over the mouthpiece on her cell and leaned toward Bear.

"We know where our Marine is."

CHAPTER TWENTY-FOUR

It took some convincing, but Sadie eventually gave in to Bear's insistence that he accompany her to track down the Marine. Winters and her available men were busy trying to stop a potential terrorist attack on the city, so Sadie would've been chasing down the lead on her own. It wasn't that Bear didn't trust her to take care of business. He just didn't like the idea that some discharged Marine was walking around the city, throwing his weight behind the very people he used to fight against.

It was personal.

Bear's wounds were fairly superficial, so the hospital couldn't hold him against his will. By the time he was released, a courier arrived from Winters to take the flash drive back to MI5 headquarters so they could start locating the tunnel that had become such a hot spot for criminal activity.

Now Sadie was speeding away from the hospital and toward the location Winters had provided her. If all went according to plan, they'd get their Marine and discover exactly how he was involved in the fire and the missing agents.

"Where are we headed?" Bear asked, adjusting his seatbelt so it didn't rub against the wounds on his chest and arm.

Sadie cast a quick glance at him before returning her eyes to the road. "I don't feel good about this, Bear. Your stitches have only been in for a couple of hours."

"I'll be fine," he said.

"I'm more worried about not having reliable backup," she said, but her voice was light.

"We both know you can handle an idiot," Bear said. "And I can still shoot a gun. I've got a couple light scratches, that's all."

"Light scratches," she repeated. Bear could practically feel her roll her eyes, but she changed the subject. "We're heading out to a private airfield. One of Miller's known aliases popped up and the owner of the airfield happens to be former military. He's stalling him until we arrive."

"That's not suspicious at all."

"Best Winters could do for now," she said. "He's alone, so hopefully he'll recognize the situation and come quietly."

"Doubtful," Bear said, "but it's good to remain positive."

Sadie offered a noncommittal sound and the two of them remained silent for the rest of the ride. Bear kept shifting uncomfortably in his seat. Aside from the obvious wounds, he had a couple killer bruises. He tried closing his eyes, but every time he was nearly asleep, they'd hit a bump in the road and he'd be once again reminded of how much pain he was in.

Luckily, they didn't have to go far. The airfield was just outside the city, close enough that hotshots could make their way to London in record time but far enough away that they wouldn't have to rub elbows with commoners as they deplaned.

Or at least that's what Bear imagined they were like. You were either rich or up to no good if you used a private airfield. He'd done it on occasion, but he usually fell into the latter category.

Their approach to the hangar was shielded by a line of trees. There was a surprising amount of forest around the big open field where the planes landed, but Bear assumed that was to help add to the whole isolation effect.

Sadie parked the car in the lot and pointed toward the building. The front office had a large window they could look into. There was a man behind a computer on one side of a desk and another man in a baseball cap and camo jacket on the other side.

"That's our guy," Sadie said. "You should stay here."

Bear was halfway out of the car already. "Why?"

"He knows who you are," Sadie said, leveling Bear with a stern gaze. "I might actually be able to get a drop on him if you're not standing next to me."

Bear gave a look but didn't argue. As much as he wanted to go toe to toe with this guy, he wasn't exactly in the best condition for a fist fight. "Fine. But if it goes sideways, I'm not going to hesitate."

"I wouldn't have it any other way."

Sadie left Bear behind and made her way toward the office. The man behind the counter glanced at her approach but his body language never gave anything away. Bear assumed he knew who Sadie was, but if he was former military, he knew enough not to tip off their target.

As for Miller, his body language was practically screaming. His arms were crossed tightly over his chest and Bear could tell he was red in the face even from his vantage point in the car. Miller likely knew he had to get out of the country fast and wasn't too happy at the excuses their man behind the counter kept coming up with.

Sadie entered the office and Bear absently moved his hand to the door handle, ready to throw it open and barge his way into the office if it looked like she was in any trouble. He had no doubt Sadie could handle herself, but they also didn't know what kind of loose cannon Miller was yet. He was clearly off his rocker, but how far was he willing to go to escape the law?

Bear had his answer soon enough.

As soon as Sadie entered the office, Miller reacted. Bear wasn't sure if he recognized Sadie, or just knew instinctively that she was there to take him in. Either way, he knocked her to the ground, grabbed a backpack that had been sitting at his feet, and barreled his way out of the room.

Miller had been heading toward the parking lot, presumably where he had parked his car, but upon looking up and seeing Bear standing next to Sadie's vehicle, he did an about-face and took off running toward the plane parked in the hangar.

Bear ran toward the office to make sure Sadie wasn't seriously injured, but she had popped back up to her feet and was shouting something at the man behind the counter. Then she threw open the office door, pulled her sidearm, and started chasing after Miller. Bear was right on her heels.

Their target had initially made his way toward the plane, but upon seeing it wasn't even ready for takeoff, he veered off to the right and made a beeline for the forest surrounding the airfield.

"We're going to lose him," Bear shouted.

"No, we're not," Sadie yelled back. She put on an extra burst of speed, and it was all Bear could do to keep up. He could feel the skin around his stitches pulling in different directions. He ignored the discomfort.

Miller headed straight into the trees. Sadie made a gesture for Bear to go right while she went left. They'd find a way to either flank him or head him off if he decided to go in one direction or another. Bear absently wondered if he had another vehicle stashed nearby or if he was just hoping to outmaneuver or outlast them. The guy had proven he could survive on the run.

Bear ignored the pain and kept his pace steady. Miller was a solid guy, but still smaller than Bear. He looked lean, but that didn't always translate to being a particularly fast or steady runner.

Sadie was already several lengths ahead of Bear. She was quick on her feet, but Bear wasn't sure about her stamina. He'd be able to stay on track for some time even if he was falling behind. They made a good team and balanced each other out.

In the distance Bear could see Miller slowing down. The man

kept his head on a swivel. He was trying to figure out what direction would give him the best chance at escaping his pursuers. He must've seen Bear further behind him out of the corner of his eye because he took a sharp turn to the right in an attempt to put more distance between him and Sadie.

But she was gaining on him. A few more minutes and she'd have him tackled to the ground.

That's when Bear's worst nightmare came true.

Miller skidded to a halt and faced his pursuers. He drew his pistol and within a second drew aim on his target. Then he lined up a shot, aiming the barrel directly at Sadie's chest, center mass, and pulled the trigger.

CHAPTER TWENTY-FIVE

S adie dove out of the way and the bullet hit the tree behind her. Bark and wood chips sprayed in all directions. Miller froze and tried to fire again, but Sadie had rolled through and took cover behind a thick oak.

Bear sprinted toward Miller. As the man turned to find his next target, Bear slammed into him. Miller managed a shot but not before Bear had control of the man's arm. Bear knocked the pistol from Miller's hand and tackled him to the ground.

Even under Bear's control, Miller never stopped moving. And he was stronger than Bear gave him credit for. Miller rolled to the side, putting Bear on his back. Then he pulled a knife from an ankle sheath and sliced at Bear's face. Bear blocked the attack, but the point of the blade was only inches from his left eye. Miller might've been half Bear's size, but he was all muscle. Bear struggled to push him off.

The sound of a gunshot made both of them freeze. Bear could've sworn he saw Miller's hair flutter in the wake of the bullet. They both turned to see Sadie on one knee, her gun trained on Miller's forehead.

"Drop the knife," she yelled out.

Miller hesitated. Bear took the opportunity to twist Miller's arms to the side, throwing him off balance and knocking the knife from his hand. Bear scrambled out of the way, just in case Sadie decided to put Miller down for good.

"Hands up," Sadie shouted. "I'm not shooting to kill, so just keep that in mind."

Miller slowly raised his hands while Bear made his way over to Sadie's side. He leaned in close to her.

"Were you trying to hit him or did you miss on purpose?"

Sadie gave an incredulous look without ever taking her eyes off their target.

"Right," Bear muttered. "Stupid question."

"Face down," Sadie called out. "Hands behind your back."

Miller followed orders. His face hardened like stone.

Sadie handed Bear a pair of handcuffs and kept her aim trained on Miller while Bear secured him. When Bear hauled the guy to his feet, Miller resisted. Bear landed a punch to his gut. Miller groaned but managed to keep himself upright.

Bear led Miller back to the office at the airfield while Sadie hung back, grabbed his backpack, and kept him in her sights. The guy had resigned himself to the situation and followed Bear's orders. Was he giving up? Or biding his time until he saw another opportunity to escape? Either way, they weren't going to take any chances.

The man behind the counter, who introduced himself as Benedict Corbyn, was surprised when they returned with Miller in tow but quickly fetched a rope they could use to secure him. When Bear was done tying Miller to a pillar in the hangar, Corbyn gestured for the three of them to huddle out of earshot.

"Not quite sure what you two are up to," Corbyn said, "but I know you're the good guys. If you need anything, let me know. Otherwise, I'll leave you to do, uh, whatever it takes."

Bear shook his hand. "Appreciate that. I'm sorry for the trouble."

Corbyn shook his head. "A patriot never stops serving their country, even when they're retired, like me."

"Thank you for your help," Sadie said, shaking his hand too. "I'll make sure we're out of your hair soon enough."

Bear waited until Corbyn walked away before turning back to Sadie. "I'm not sure I believe him."

Sadie's eyebrows pinched together. "About what?"

"About how patriots never stop serving their country." Bear hooked a thumb over his shoulder. "Just look at Miller."

"He was never a patriot," Sadie said. "He only ever served himself. He wanted violence and he got it overseas."

"Until he didn't," Bear said. "And then he found other ways to get his fix."

"Exactly." Sadie stood a little taller, squaring her shoulders in the process. "Come on. Let's get this done."

The two of them walked up to Miller, who had been struggling against his bonds while they were having their private conversation. He stilled when they stopped in front of him and leveled a glare at Sadie.

"I'm feeling a lot of hostility emanating from you, Mr. Miller," she said. "There's no need for that. I'd like this to be a quick, civilized conversation."

"He's just pissed he missed his shot," Bear said. They had never decided on playing good cop, bad cop, but he fell into the role with ease. "Twice."

"Got you, though," Miller said, turning to Bear. There was a subtle Southern twang to his voice. "Nearly took out your eye."

"I'm lucky my friend here is a better shot than you, then," Bear said. He didn't have any problem admitting Miller got the best of him, especially if it got under the other man's skin. Besides, the fight had only just begun.

"Untie me and let's go again," Miller spat. "Bet you won't be so lucky next time."

"There's not going to be a next time, so you two can stop comparing dick sizes." Sadie stared down Miller until she regained his attention. "We're less interested in you than who you work for."

"Not a chance," he said. "I'm no snitch."

"Too bad," Bear said, stepping closer. "Because one way or another we're going to find out what you've been up to and why."

"Is this where you tell me I can choose the easy way or the hard way?" Miller grinned.

Bear landed a blow against Miller's cheek. "I can't see any reason why anyone would give a lowlife piece of shit like you an option. There's only one way to do this."

Sadie held up her hand stopping Bear mid-strike. "Look, I'm going to be straight with you. You're in deep shit. We know who you are. We know you were discharged from the military under less than desirable conditions. It didn't take a genius to figure out what you got up to once you were back home."

Miller laughed. "Clearly."

Sadie ignored him. "We've got you at the scene of a crime and can tie you to a larger conspiracy. You're gonna do time. It's up to you how much."

"What crime scene?" Miller asked. He looked calm despite his predicament. "What conspiracy?"

"We know you set fire to the apartment building that was once used as a safe house for the CIA. One of them was found dead inside. Even if you didn't pull the trigger, and I'm not totally convinced you didn't, you'll be charged with obstruction of justice."

"Not such a big deal," Bear continued, "unless you factor in that those agents were part of a bigger conspiracy. We're talking terrorism, which is going to make things a lot worse for you."

For the first time, Miller looked uncomfortable. He shifted against the pillar to get better footing. "You can't prove any of that."

"Actually, we can," Sadie said. "We've got a couple of witnesses, plenty of physical evidence, and more dead bodies than we know what to do with."

"We're not interested in you," Bear said. "You're not even chicken shit to us. You're the little white speck on top of chicken shit. We want to know where the other two agents are and we want to know where the terrorists have been holed up. You help us with that, and we have no problem working to get you a nice roommate in your institution of choice. It beats the alternative."

"Which is what, exactly?"

"You take the fall for all of this." Sadie sounded nonchalant, but Bear could see the fire in her. "I have no problem weaving a very convincing tale about how you were the point man for all of this. Our judicial system will have no problem believing that a disillusioned soldier who hates his country decided to get into bed with a bunch of terrorists to teach the government a lesson. We've got dead and missing CIA agents, a brand-new militant organization, and plenty of motive to up the ante by taking those plans to bomb a tunnel Stateside."

Miller was turning red in the face. "I don't hate my country."

"Believe it or not, I know that." Sadie spread her arms wide. "But someone's gotta go down for all of this, and right now you're on point."

Miller looked between Bear and Sadie for several seconds before he spoke again. "Say I was coerced, what then?"

"Bullshit," Bear said.

Sadie held up her hand and motioned for Miller to continue.

Miller threw Bear a sly grin. "Maybe a big shot CIA agent got into contact with me and I felt it was my patriotic duty to help him out. It was too late before I realized something sinister was going on."

Sadie exchanged a look with Bear before she returned to Miller. "I'm listening."

CHAPTER TWENTY-SIX

"Start at the beginning," Bear said. He didn't like that they were entertaining the idea that Miller was spinning this to make him look like a victim, but if it led them to the big fish, it would be worth it. Miller was still going to go down for his part in the deal, and that would have to be enough.

"I'd been doing odd jobs here and there. Got most of them through mutual friends. Some of them were legit, others teetered on the line of legality." Miller smiled, but neither Sadie nor Bear reacted. "Then one day I got a call from this guy named Weber who wanted me to travel overseas for a job."

"Was that normal?" Bear asked. "To go overseas?"

Miller shrugged as best he could while still tied to the pillar in the hangar. "It's happened on occasion. Nothing as big as this, though. He told me I might be gone for a while."

"And you accepted the job, just like that?" Bear asked.

"Like I said, most of these jobs came through from mutual friends, important people. They were people I trusted. Plus, I was bored. Hadn't done anything in a while. Needed to get out of the house."

"So, you thought planning a terrorist attack was a good alternative?" Sadie asked.

"Oh, I had no idea that's what this was going to turn into," Miller said. His face was a mask of mock innocence. "By the time I realized what it truly was, it was too late."

Bear bit his tongue to keep from derailing the story. Luckily, Miller didn't notice.

"Who was the friend?" Sadie asked.

"Nah, I'm not going to tell you that. Gotta protect my contacts."

"It could only help you," Sadie said. "Think about it. If your friend is important, if he's legitimate, it'll be much easier to convince a court you had no idea what you were getting into."

For the first time Miller looked like he was taking this seriously. "I doubt he even knew about the job. He was just a waypoint for Weber and I to meet and ensure we could trust each other."

"Even better," Sadie said. "If he didn't know about the job, he could act as a character witness."

Miller looked between Bear and Sadie for a moment. Bear saw the moment when he decided to spill the beans. What he wasn't expecting was the name that dropped from Miller's mouth.

"Daniel Thorne."

Sadie stepped in before Bear even had a chance to react. "Even better. Thorne's a friend of ours, too."

Miller looked surprised. "Yeah?"

She nodded. Almost convinced Bear she was telling the truth, too. "We're both CIA. We've worked together in the past."

"Thorne's a good guy." Any trace of the cockiness from before had left Miller. "He's watched out for me over the years."

Bear couldn't stop himself from asking, "And Thorne had no idea why you were being summoned to London?"

Miller shook his head. "He's a busy guy. Has much more important things going on. Haven't seen him in a while, but if Weber knew him, then I knew I was in good hands."

Bear decided not to point out the fallacies in that statement.

Maybe Weber knew of Thorne and just name-dropped someone he knew that would get Miller to believe they were on the same side. If that were the case, then Miller hopped on the plane under false pretenses. Not that it made up for anything he had done since.

But Bear knew the truth. It was much more likely that Thorne was involved in all of this from the beginning. And now they could link Thorne with everything going on with the missing agents through both Maria and Miller.

Sadie didn't meet Bear's eyes after the revelation and Bear followed her lead. They'd be much more likely to get information out of Miller if he believed they were on Thorne's side. The guy clearly had a lot of respect for Thorne, and they were going to use that to their advantage for as long as they could.

"What happened once you got to England?" Sadie asked.

"Met up with Weber, whose real name was actually Fredericks."

Sadie turned to Bear for the first time. "One of our missing agents."

Miller settled into the story. "He told me he was on the job, but that he was running a side scheme he needed some extra help with. His team was supposed to be keeping an eye on a terrorist cell that had popped up in London recently. He and his team were monitoring them until they were ready to make their first move. Once they did, the CIA would catch them in the act and come home heroes."

"And the side scheme?" Bear asked.

"They knew the terrorist cell was planning on using an underground tunnel to plant bombs and cause some serious destruction. But they'd also gotten wind of a local gang that was eying the same territory. Fredericks figured he could go to both of them and offer to look the other way—for a price."

"He was double-dipping," Sadie said. "Neither one had any idea the other existed, and while they thought they'd be able to operate under law enforcement's noses, Fredericks would collect money from both sides before they ever figured out what he was doing."

"Except they were both pretty suspicious to begin with," Miller said, "so he brought me in to keep the peace. Of course, at the time I thought I was meeting with legitimate businessmen, not gang leaders and terrorists. Once we convinced each of them to take the deal, Fredericks had me call a phone number and drop a tip about the terrorist cell's plans. Then his team could swoop in and save the day."

"Why just the terrorists?" Bear asked. "Why not the gang, too?"

"Don't know," Miller said. "I can't imagine Fredericks really wanting a terrorist cell to run rampant here or anywhere else. As for the gang, maybe he figured he could keep getting hush money out of them? All they wanted to do was sell drugs. Not quite as big a deal as blowing up some building in the middle of a major city."

"Tell that to all the orphaned kids wondering what happened to their coked-up parents," Sadie said.

Miller shrugged and looked like he didn't care.

"So where did things go wrong?" Bear asked.

"Like I said, I called the number he gave me, talked to some girl. Gave her the tip and stuck around long enough to watch the fireworks. Only, instead of watching Fredericks and his boys being congratulated on a job well done by the Queen, I find out they all went missing and now the Irish and the Arabs are at each other's necks."

"So, you decided to burn the apartment building down to cover your own ass?" Bear asked.

"Not at first," Miller said. "Fredericks still hadn't given me my cut, so I waited for him to turn up again. Kept my ear to the ground in case he had taken off hoping to get one over on me. About a week went by and I saw one of the terrorist guys dumping a body in the apartment. Went to go check it out and realized it was one of Fredericks' men."

"Were either of them in on the deal?" Sadie asked.

"Nah. They were straight shooters. It seemed to drive Fredericks crazy. That's why he brought me in. Knew he couldn't trust them to keep their mouths shut."

"Who was in the apartment?" Bear asked.

"Sheehan. He was already dead." Miller's voice grew angry. "I didn't sign up for that shit. Dead CIA agent? Nah, I wasn't going to go down for that."

"So you decided to scrub the apartment," Bear said. "Set everything on fire, destroy the evidence."

"Figured someone would come looking for them eventually, and the less that tied me to whatever happened, the better. So, yeah, I set fire to the place."

"And almost killed a lot of people in the process, including an innocent kid."

Miller shifted uncomfortably against the pillar. "Look, that wasn't my intention. I figured he was with someone. Figured someone would smell the gas and pull the alarm before anything bad happened."

"You have a lot of faith in people," Bear said. "You took a big chance there."

"Seemed to work out, though, didn't it?"

Bear gritted his teeth. Miller was right, but he wasn't going to give him the satisfaction of admitting that out loud.

"Here's the million-dollar question," Sadie said. "Where's Fredericks and the other agent?"

"Hell if I know," Miller said. "If Fredericks is smart, he's far away from here. Maybe he's holed up with his girlfriend."

"Girlfriend?" Bear asked. "Who?"

Miller shrugged. "I don't know. Some red-haired chick. I think she was the one I talked to on the phone. The one who got the tip and gave it to the whole team."

Sadie stiffened. "You remember her name?"

"Mary," Miller said. "No, wait. It was Maria."

CHAPTER TWENTY-SEVEN

Bear waited until they were out of earshot of Miller before he turned to Sadie. "What the fuck is going on here?"

Sadie closed her eyes and put her hands on the side of her head, like she was trying to keep her mind from spilling out of her ears. "From the very beginning everything has been so tied up with everything else. How did we not see it?"

"See what?" Bear demanded. He felt spittle fly from his lips. "Because all I see is a clusterfuck of epic proportions. I mean, Thorne? Maria? They've been involved in this from the beginning?"

"Hang on, hang on," Sadie said. "Let me get this straight in my head."

Bear bit down on his tongue to keep from lashing out. He had a lot of pent-up energy and absolutely no outlet for it. He looked back at Miller, who appeared to be trying to take a nap standing up, now that his interrogation was done. Maybe Bear could beat more information out of him.

"Thorne knew both Fredericks and Miller, who teamed up to double-cross a terrorist cell and an Irish gang here in London. Miller called Maria, who was working for Thorne at the time, to give her a tip about the terrorist cell. When all that went sideways, our three agents disappeared. Sheehan showed up dead at the apartment building, and Miller decided to burn it to the ground to cover his tracks. But Fredericks and the third agent, Samson, are still missing."

"And we know the neo jihadists still have them," Bear said.

Sadie finally opened her eyes. "That's got to be why Maria decided to go back and check on the agents. She wasn't worried about following up on potential bad intel. She wanted to know what happened to her boyfriend. He'd been missing and she knew something was wrong."

"She could've been in on the deal," Bear said. "If she knew he was dirty, she was probably helping him. And if she knew—"

"Then Thorne knew, too."

Bear scrubbed a hand across his face. "We need to talk to Thorne."

Sadie shook her head. "I'm not kicking that hornet's nest yet. I want to know everything I can before we knock on that door."

"You want to talk to Maria first."

Sadie nodded. "And we're not doing any of that computer bullshit, either. I want her here. Now."

Bear didn't argue. He could feel the waves of anticipation rolling off of Sadie, and they matched his own. Sadie stepped away to make a phone call while Bear returned to Miller.

"What happened to you, man?" Bear asked. "Seriously. You were willing to kill so many people, and for what? A paycheck?"

Miller's eyes burned. "Retribution pays a lot more than money."

"You fought over there for years. Fought to protect your country. And now you're helping those same people destroy the world."

Miller clenched his teeth, but Bear saw the beginning of a crack in his façade. "It wasn't supposed to be like that. No one was supposed to get hurt."

"But there was a chance all this could go sideways, and then you'd be part of a terrorist plot."

"Look, I know I've been a piece of shit for most of my life." Miller wasn't meeting Bear's eyes. "I could've been a better soldier. A better son, too. I've been so angry most of my life. At everything. Everyone. Figured I could put that to good use. But even over there, it wasn't just about putting down the bad guy. There were rules and expectations."

"Go figure. How dare the military hold you to a higher standard."

Miller wasn't taking the bait. "When they discharged me, I thought my life was over. Nearly did it myself a few times. Then I started finding ways to put my skills to work. I helped some people too, you know. I doubt that'll be in my file when all is said and done."

"Even if it is, you've hurt more than you helped."

Miller's sigh was one of resignation. "We were supposed to be the heroes. Fredericks was gonna bring me in on the takedown job. I wanted the money, don't get me wrong, but he thought maybe this could get me back in. The Marines. The CIA. Something. He thought I could start over."

Bear felt the slightest hint of pity for the man, but everything he'd done squashed that fairly quickly. "And now you'll need to figure out how to redeem yourself from inside a jail cell."

Miller hung his head and didn't answer. What could he say? Both he and Bear knew it was over for him. The best he could hope for was a lenient sentence, a decent prison, and a life on the inside where he could fly under the radar.

Bear didn't have high hopes, but he at least gave Miller the courtesy of not telling him that.

Sadie walked over to them, tucking her phone back in her pocket. "You're all set, Mr. Miller. A team is gonna pick you up and take you back to the States. They're going to listen to what you have to say. I suggest you tell them the truth. I'm willing to back you up if you do. They'll know you helped us. It won't let you off the hook, but it'll get you far enough."

"Thank you." Miller's cocky attitude hadn't returned.

"He's feeling remorseful at the moment," Bear said once they were out of earshot. "Let's hope it lasts."

"Indeed." Sadie motioned for Bear to follow her. "We've got moves to make."

After ensuring Miller was secure, they left him in the care of Mr. Corbyn, who promised to keep an eye on him until the team arrived. Bear wasn't sure how he felt about leaving Miller behind without seeing him picked up with his own two eyes, but Sadie was on a mission.

"I called Langley," she said. They were both in her car again, making their way back to London. "Gave them the basics on the situation, including my thoughts on Maria and Thorne."

"Which are?" Bear asked.

"Something is going on here."

"That's it?" Bear laughed. "That's all we're going on?"

"It was enough for Langley," Sadie said. "They know what Thorne is capable of. They're not taking any chances."

"Did you ask if he's still in his cell? I wouldn't put it past him."

"He's there," Sadie said. "I had them look before I got off the phone."

Bear cracked the window and let the cool air wash over his face for a moment. "I half expected them to find a bunch of pillows stuffed under his covers."

"A mop for hair," Sadie said, laughing. "Me, too."

"Jesus." Bear didn't know what else to say. "I'm gonna need to go on some blood pressure medication after this, you know that, right?"

"You're getting too old for this, Bear. You need to leave it to us young kids."

"My ass," Bear said, but there wasn't the usual heat behind his words. He turned to look at Sadie, who had her eyes fixed on the road. "You ever get tired?"

"We all need to sleep, Bear."

"That's not what I mean and you know it."

Sadie twisted her mouth to the side, but it looked more like a grimace than a smile. "I don't know. Sometimes. But then I get a new mission and I feel like a new person again, you know? I love what I do, Bear. I can't imagine doing anything else."

"That'll change."

Sadie laughed. "Now you really do sound like an old man."

"Yeah," Bear said. He looked out the window. "I feel it sometimes, too."

There was a beat of silence between them before Sadie spoke again. "What's going on in that head of yours, Bear? You've been off this entire trip."

"I don't know."

"I think you do, but you don't want to say it out loud."

Bear turned back to her. "Woman's intuition?"

"That and I have eyes," Sadie said, meeting his gaze for a moment before returning to the road.

"Jack and I have been on our own before. We don't run every mission together. But this feels different. Something feels wrong."

"I know what you mean," Sadie said. "It's like he's trying to ask us for help but doesn't know how."

"And I just keeping thinking, how long can one person do this? Most of us are dead or called by forty. Don't get a chance to feel tired. And those who retire are always jumping back into the game. They always have their head on a swivel."

"And if they weren't crazy before, they will be eventually." She laughed. "Yeah, I think about that, too."

"Our bodies can only take so much excitement before they give out," Bear said.

"You falling apart, big man?" Sadie asked.

"Not yet." Bear's voice was sober. "But I can feel it coming. And Jack? He takes bigger risks than I do. It's only a matter of time. I just keep wondering—should I be spending the rest of my days doing this? Chasing down terrorists and gangs and missing agents?"

"What do you want instead? A white picket fence? A wife and kids?"

"You mean a life?" Bear laughed. "I don't know, maybe. Sometimes. It would be nice to have a home to go back to."

"You have a place, don't you?"

"A place, yeah." Bear could hear his voice turn wistful. "But not a home."

"And the wife and kids?"

"I could do it. I could enjoy that life."

"But?" Sadie asked. "I feel a *but* coming on."

"But I'd always be worried. You think I'm paranoid now? Shit, wait till I've got a son or daughter to take care of."

"Do you think it'd be worth it? The paranoia, I mean, just to have a family?"

"Yeah, sometimes I do."

Sadie changed lanes before she answered. "You're allowed to call it whenever you want to, Bear. That's well within your rights."

"I know." When Sadie gave him a look like she didn't believe it, he continued. "Really, I know that. But I also know what's out there. How could I stand by and do nothing knowing everything I know?"

"You can't save everybody," Sadie said. "It's a hard lesson to learn, but a necessary one. Even now, there are a hundred other terrorist plots being concocted around the world. Some of them will be stopped by other teams. Some of them will change the course of history. We do what we can until we can't even do that anymore. There's no shame in hanging it up, Bear. Especially if it keeps you alive."

Bear nodded, but he wasn't sure he felt the same way.

"I hate seeing you like this," Sadie said.

"I'll be fine," Bear said.

"I know that. I just wish *you* did."

CHAPTER TWENTY-EIGHT

B ear woke up the following day feeling well-rested but no less exhausted by recent events.

As much as he didn't want to admit it, this trip had taken a toll on him. He'd been up the whole night before, first tracking down Seamus, then getting into a fight with the neo jihadists, and finally locating and interrogating Miller. His body had been ready for some sleep, even if he had trouble turning off his brain.

By the time Sadie had collected him at his hotel, he was conscious, but no readier to tackle the day ahead of them.

"You don't look like you got much sleep," he said.

Sadie took a long sip of her coffee while keeping an eye on the road in front of them. "Got a couple hours, but it's been a busy night."

"Give me the short version," Bear said, settling back into his seat and closing his eyes. They were still heavy with exhaustion.

"Filled Winters in on the situation. She's still trying to track down the tunnel in question. It seems like the cell isn't aware we know as much as we do, otherwise they would've sent another video or blown it up at this point."

"Let's hope we can catch them before they move on to Plan B," Bear said. There was a beat of silence between them before Bear broke it as nonchalantly as he could. "So, we haven't really talked about it yet."

"Talked about what?"

"The fact that one of your men was dirty."

Sadie sighed and waited until they got off the highway before she answered. "It's never a great feeling, but I know it wasn't my fault. I did everything by the book. Fredericks was a good agent. Dependable. Courageous. He had quite a few years in before he joined my team. There was no way I could've known."

"Is Langley going to see it that way?"

Sadie laughed. "That's the question, isn't it? There will be an inquiry, but I doubt I'll get anything more than a stern talking-to."

"Good for you."

"Bad for Fredericks," Sadie said. "His career is over. That's if he's still alive."

"That was *his* call," Bear said. "He chose to get greedy."

"I'm more interested in Maria anyway," Sadie said. "I keep underestimating her and it's starting to get on my nerves."

Bear was kicking himself, too. "She knew a lot more than she first let on, that's for sure."

"Now we just have to figure out how much of it was Thorne and how much of it was because she got a crush on the guy she was supposed to be keeping an eye on."

"How are we going to approach this one?"

"Bad cop, bad cop," Sadie said. There was no hesitation. "I'm tired of the runaround. Langley picked her up last night and put her on a plane. She's been at MI5 headquarters for a couple hours now. I told them to keep her comfortable but to leave her alone until we got there."

"She's going to know something is up," Bear said.

"I'm counting on it," Sadie said. "The more on edge she is, the more likely we'll be able to crack her."

"Are you sure about that?" Bear asked. "If she's as tight with Thorne as we think she is, she'll know all our tricks. She might clam up instead."

"And we've underestimated her in the past," Sadie admitted. "But we've played nice before and she walked all over us. Time to confront her head-on."

Bear didn't argue and they remained silent for the rest of the ride to HQ. It didn't take long, but he was aware that every minute was one step closer to the inevitable. They had one day left before their deadline was up. Fredericks might be a traitor to his country, but Bear still felt it was his duty to find him and the other agent, Samson.

By the time they arrived at HQ and were escorted to the interview room where Maria was being kept, Bear was ready to get some answers. He thought back to when he first met her—dirty, injured, and so drugged up she could barely function. He thought finding out she was working with Thorne was betrayal enough, but what if she had never stopped working for him? What if all of this was part of Thorne's master plan, even from the beginning?

Bear was really tired of being a cog in someone else's machine.

Sadie entered first, with Bear close behind. Maria, still a redhead, sat at the table cradling a cup of coffee in her hands. She was in an oversized sweater and leggings. The agents who brought her in had been instructed not to use force or handcuffs unless absolutely necessary. From what Sadie had heard, Maria hadn't really put up much of a fight.

"Good morning," Sadie said, not bothering to smile.

"Is it?" Maria asked. Upon closer inspection, Bear noticed her hair was tousled and she had dark circles under her eyes. "I didn't really sleep well last night."

"I'm sorry for having to put you on a plane like that."

"It's fine," Maria said, and she looked like she meant it. "I want to help, but they didn't really tell me much. What's going on? Did you find the other two agents?"

"Not yet," Sadie said. She sat down across from Maria, and Bear joined her. "We're hoping you can give us some more information."

"I basically told you everything I know," Maria said. Her gaze was earnest and Bear had to remind himself she was lying. Thorne had taught her better than they all thought. Took her natural abilities and enhanced them.

"That's not quite true." Sadie leaned back in her chair and crossed her arms. "You never told us about your relationship with Agent Fredericks."

Maria froze and her eyes went wide for a split second before she regained her composure. Bear could practically feel her brain scrambling for an excuse.

"I didn't mean to keep that from you."

"But you did." Bear couldn't stop himself from sounding disappointed.

"I knew it was inappropriate," Maria said. She slid her cup farther away from her and placed her palms flat on the table. "I honestly didn't think it had anything to do with them going missing, so I... Wait a minute, do you think I killed that agent? That I kidnapped the others?"

"No," Sadie said. "No, we don't think that. But it's clear you were involved somehow."

"Now would be a good time to come clean, Maria," Bear said.

Maria sat up straighter. "Everything I told you is true. Thorne sent me there to help keep the agents informed. I was meant to sound local, so as to not raise suspicion. I was meant to get close to them to gain their trust. All they knew about me was that I had access to information. They took advantage of my connections."

"How close were you meant to get?" Sadie asked.

"Nothing was supposed to develop between us," Maria said. "I've had missions like that before and it wasn't meant to go down in that way. But Aaron and I just sort of hit it off."

"And you didn't think that could compromise the mission?" Sadie asked. Bear could hear the criticism in her voice.

"No," Maria said, sitting back. It seemed like she could hear it, too. "No, of course not. What we did outside of the information exchange had no bearing on the mission. They were still doing their jobs and I was still doing mine."

"But when you went back to check on the agents, it was for personal reasons," Bear said.

Maria chewed on her bottom lip before she answered. "I knew something was wrong because I hadn't heard from him in a while. When I couldn't figure out where he went, I got in contact with you."

"How did you know he wasn't just blowing you off?" Sadie asked.

Maria's face turned red. "He wouldn't do that."

"You didn't know him for very long," Bear pointed out. "How can you be sure?"

"Look, I didn't love him or anything," Maria said. "I knew what it was. But we were honest with each other. We knew it wasn't going to last. But he would've told me if he was leaving. He would've said goodbye."

"If you were honest with each other, then he would've told you about his side business," Sadie said.

Maria opened her mouth and closed it, but she couldn't form any words.

"He either lied to you, Maria, or you lied to us. Which one is it?"

When she remained silent, Bear leaned forward. "Whoever you're trying to protect, just remember they're not the ones in the hot seat right now. You are. I understand loyalty, trust me. But at the end of the day, you have to look out for yourself first and foremost."

"It was Thorne's idea," Maria said after a moment. Her voice had dropped half an octave. The innocent act was over.

Bear sat up straighter. "What was?"

"He knew Fredericks was dirty. This isn't the first time he pulled a scheme like this. He wanted me to get close to him, to figure out how we could use him to either get in on his schemes or blackmail him. Thorne didn't really care which."

"Why didn't you tell us about this from the beginning?" Sadie asked.

The tears in Maria's eyes might've been the first real ones Bear had seen from her. "I was scared."

"Of what?"

"Of him," Maria said. "Of Thorne. Who else?"

"He's locked up," Bear said. "He's going to be in there for a long time."

Maria shook her head. "He's going to get out. I know he is. Part of me hopes he does, that he'll come for me. And the other part..."

"Is worried he won't," Sadie said. Her voice told Bear she understood what Maria was feeling in that moment, even if he was having trouble grasping the scope of it.

Maria nodded, tears still streaming down her face.

"Thorne doesn't care about you, Maria," Bear said. "You know that. He proved that the last time you two were working together."

"I know." Maria wiped her tears on her sleeves and tried to get her voice under control, but it was still shaky. "I know that. I'm not stupid. I know what kind of person he is. I was just sort of hoping I was the exception to the rule."

Sadie nodded her head. "He made you feel special, and then you found out he saw you the same way he sees everyone else. I've been there. I know how difficult that is to process. It's going to take a long time to get over those feelings of betrayal and worthlessness, but you can do it. I did it. I can help you."

Maria looked up at Sadie, her eyes still wet with tears. "I'm scared."

"I know." Sadie reached out and put a hand on Maria's arm. "But the only way you're going to heal is by moving on from him. And the only way you can ensure that is if you tell us everything you know about why he was interested in Fredericks in the first place. You've got all the power this time, Maria. I trust that you can use it to do the right thing. Can you do that? Can you do that for yourself?"

Maria swallowed and took a shaky breath. When she met Sadie's eyes, Bear noticed a fierce determination there.

"I can do that."

CHAPTER TWENTY-NINE

Sadie had someone bring Maria a bottle of water and some tissues. After a few minutes to gather herself, Maria's voice no longer shook when she spoke.

"Thorne has a network of people from all over the world that he uses to carry out his own personal business. Agents, criminals, government workers, ordinary people. It doesn't matter who they are, but it does matter what they do."

Bear had so many questions, but he was afraid that if he spoke, it would break the spell and Maria would stop divulging information.

"Some of them are like-minded people. Others have been bought out. Some have been blackmailed. I'm pretty sure there are even some who have no idea they're part of a larger scheme. Thorne is smart and charming. He can get anyone to do anything he wants."

Maria took a moment to sip her water.

"He wanted Fredericks on his team. I was meant to get close to him so I could find out what sort of approach was needed. Could Fredericks be bought out, and if so, would it be worth it? Or was blackmail a better option? I thought I was handling the situation just fine until another one of Thorne's assets showed up."

"Who?" Sadie asked.

"I didn't catch his name, but I know he was former military. He never rubbed me the right way."

"His name was Miller," Bear said. "What seemed off about him?"

"He was like a bull in a china shop. I was worried he'd blow the whole thing. I don't think he knew I was with Thorne either. Kept bragging about how his boss was untouchable, and that meant he was untouchable, too. I wasn't really sure what Thorne saw in him."

"You were jealous," Sadie said, gently.

Maria opened her mouth, clearly intending to argue, but nodded her head instead. "I worked so hard to have Thorne put his trust in me. And this guy waltzes in like he's better than me?"

"Different people have different purposes," Sadie said. "It doesn't mean Thorne thought any less of you."

"I guess." Maria brushed away another tear before continuing. "Either way, I knew Thorne was testing me. He'd been hands-off on my missions for a while now, but he went dark this time around. I was supposed to figure out what needed to be done and handle it on my own. The Marine was a wrench in the system. I knew I was supposed to handle it on top of my assignment."

"All of the newspaper articles you had looked through when you got the anonymous tip were fake," Sadie said. Her voice was still gentle, cautious. "And the tip came from Miller himself."

Maria's mouth hardened. "Guess I should've known that."

"It might've been a test," Bear said, "but that didn't make it any less real. The terrorist cell exists."

"But the tip implied they had planted bombs already. That wasn't true. This tunnel job was going to be the first one," Sadie said. "No one knew about these neo jihadists until the agents disappeared."

"Thorne did," Bear said. "He told Miller to phone in the tip. He knew about them."

"So, was he trying to help us by informing the CIA and eventually MI5 of the new cell?"

"Nothing is ever that straightforward with Thorne," Bear said.

"He's not a bad person," Maria said. When both Sadie and Bear raised their eyebrows at her, she rushed on. "I know that makes me seem crazier than I already am, but Thorne isn't evil. He doesn't always do the right thing, sure, but that doesn't make him a bad guy. He just lives in a gray world. He sees things differently than we do."

Sadie's gentle voice was in full effect now. "This job requires you to visit that gray area from time to time, but Thorne has been living there for far too long. After a while, those lines start to blend and you begin making the wrong calls. It happens to good agents all the time."

Maria bowed her head.

"What did Thorne want to accomplish by putting Fredericks and his team on the trail of the neo jihadists?" Bear asked.

When Maria didn't offer any explanation, Sadie started thinking out loud. "For one, he knew Fredericks was dirty, so Thorne wanted to see if he'd take the bait and set up a deal. From what we know, Fredericks was never going to let the terrorist plot go down after he got his money. Thorne likely knew that, so this seems like a two-birds-one-stone situation."

"Get Fredericks on his team and take out the cell in the process," Bear said.

"Exactly." Sadie ran her fingers through her hair. "But when it went sideways, he was nowhere to be found."

"After he was caught, I went back to check in on Fredericks hoping I could secure the deal with him," Maria admitted. "When I realized he was missing, I knew my best bet was getting help to track him down. Thorne had a backup plan, like always, but I was hoping it wouldn't come down to that."

"A backup plan?" Bear asked.

Maria took another sip of water before answering. "If I failed to secure the deal, or if something went wrong, the cell still needed to be taken care of. He had a special asset who was going to come in and wipe everything clean."

"What kind of asset?" Sadie asked.

"I honestly don't know. Thorne didn't tell me anything. No

name. No details. Nothing. But it sounded like a big deal. Like someone really dangerous."

"Great," Bear said, leaning back in his chair. "Another player on the board to keep an eye out for."

Sadie opened her mouth to speak when there was a sharp knock on the door. Director Winters walked in without waiting for an answer. She glanced at Maria before settling her gaze on Sadie and Bear.

"A word?" Winters asked.

Sadie and Bear followed Winters out into the hallway. Sadie waited for the door to close behind them before taking an aggressive step toward the Director.

"We could've been in the middle of a pivotal part of an interrogation. Your disruption could've cost us the entire interview."

"I waited as long as I could. I didn't do this lightly." Winters handed Sadie a manila envelope. "But considering these were your men, I figured you'd want to know, regardless."

"Know what?" Bear asked, watching as Sadie opened the envelope and pulled a stack of papers out.

"We found them," Winters announced. "The terrorists and the missing agents. We know where they are."

CHAPTER THIRTY

B ear found himself sitting in the back of a van with Sadie and a handful of Director Winters' best operatives from the anti-terrorism division. One was driving the vehicle, while the others were taking time to double check their weapons and secure their gear.

For his part, Bear was working with a borrowed vest and helmet, but it fit well enough. Maybe on the snug side. He was used to running into bad situations even with his best hopes and prayers, so it was nice to have a little extra padding between him and the bullets that were surely headed his way.

He looked over at Sadie, who was loading her MP-5. "You good?" he asked.

"Better than ever," she said. "Ready to bring our boys home."

Despite Winters' untimely interruption, Sadie had jumped at the opportunity to be a part of the team to take down the neo jihadist cell and get the two CIA agents back safely. They were about twelve hours out from their deadline, and there was no guarantee Fredericks and Samson were still alive.

Bear and Sadie had been filled in on the details while they loaded up a couple vans and headed out. Between the information they had recovered from the flash drive and further interrogation of the Irish gang, Winters had tracked down the tunnel everyone had tried to claim as their own. It was an abandoned underground track from several decades ago. The rock wasn't stable enough to host constant train travel, so the project had been written off as a total loss.

But it hadn't even been closed off to the public. If you had a flashlight and some time on your hands, you could get to the area without much trouble. It was out of the way enough to remain fairly untouched but close enough to other major connections to be the perfect crossroads to stash drugs.

Or plant a bomb.

By the time the van rolled to a stop, the team of about twelve men and women were ready to move on command. Sadie and Bear had assured Winters they wouldn't have any problem falling in line, and when Agent Gerald Davis, a graying man with a beard and piercing blue eyes, gave them a command, the two Americans did as they were told.

Working with a team you're familiar with is paramount when you're trying to be safe and decisive. Bear and Sadie were at a disadvantage here, so they brought up the rear, making sure they didn't step on any toes along the way. The rest of the agents were courteous but business-like. This was personal for everyone. London was their city, and even though Fredericks and Samson weren't their men, this was a brotherhood. Everyone had skin in the game.

But Bear did wonder how much the agents knew about their current situation. He was sure Davis was filled in on every detail, but what about the others? Were they aware that Fredericks was dirty? Did that make them less inclined to put in their all? They were professionals, but they were also human. Could he fault them for holding a grudge?

When the team unloaded from the two vans, the agents formed two separate lines, with Sadie at the end of one and Bear at the end of the other. Davis made sure they were all set before he offered them a quick and efficient pep talk.

"We don't know what we're getting into here," he said, making sure he locked eyes with each and every one of them. "The stakes are about as high as they come. Intel told us this was the door to knock on, but we don't know if anyone is home. Normally we'd sit on that until we were sure, but with a countdown clock, that's not in the stars for us."

Davis walked back to the front of the group. "We've got two foreign exchange students with us here today. But just because they're new doesn't mean we need to coddle them. They come highly recommended by the Director. Today, they're one of ours. They'll watch our backs and we'll watch theirs. Is that understood?"

Everyone on the team answered in the affirmative. Bear felt that swell of community that always came with being part of a team. It'd been a while for him, but he never forgot how good it felt to know your brothers and sisters had your back.

"Then let's move out," Davis said.

The twelve men and women put one foot in front of the other without hesitation. Bear and Sadie exchanged a look and a nod, and that encapsulated everything that needed to be said. If one of them went down, at least they knew everything was out in the air between them.

The entrance to the abandoned tunnel started as an offshoot from a working train station, which meant quite a few civilians got the scare of a lifetime when two teams of armed agents descended the staircase and made their way along the platform as one cohesive unit. Most people scattered, choosing to leave the station altogether rather than risk sticking around for the show.

Winters had called ahead and gotten the trains to stop running for a short amount of time. It wasn't public knowledge, so the platform was still flooded, but it mostly cleared out by the time the team was jumping down onto the tracks and making their way deeper into the tunnel.

Bear kept his ears open for anything that didn't sound like it belonged. Despite the fact that they were all walking as softly as they could in their boots, their footsteps echoed off the tunnel walls. As much as he wanted the neo jihadists and their captives to be home so they could put an end to this entire situation, Bear was afraid they'd hear them coming and the missing agents would pay the price.

Despite the fact that he knew the tracks were momentarily shut down, Bear couldn't help keeping his ears particularly tuned to the sound of the trains moving back and forth on the tracks. There was little room on either side of the tunnel to press yourself against the wall if something went wrong. And he wasn't exactly the smallest member of the group.

Luckily, the first door on their right was the golden ticket. Davis pulled it open while two of his guys walked in, their guns raised and steady. They cleared the room and called out quietly that it was safe for them to move forward. Bear and Sadie double-checked the tunnel behind them to make sure they weren't being followed, and then allowed the door to shut silently behind them.

Inside, the group formed a single line and wound their way through a narrow back tunnel. Winters had told them this was the only way in and out of the abandoned tunnel. Years of graffiti and empty bottles told Bear that bored teenagers had discovered the area and probably used it as a party spot. Until the new neighbors moved in.

The group was met with another door, which was treated exactly the same as the last one. Davis opened it, two agents went through first, quietly called out the all clear, and the rest of the team funneled through the narrow opening.

The tunnel here was somehow even darker than the last one. Although all of them had lights attached to their weapons, the darkness seemed to suck the brightness away. Bear could hardly see five feet in front of him. He was surrounded by dripping water and rustling rats and a strange stale wind. It made the hair on the back of his neck stand on end.

Were they surrounded or was he just being paranoid?

Bear shook off the feeling and watched Davis signal the team to split off against opposite sides of the tunnel. They pushed forward, as silent as the crunch of gravel and debris would allow them to be. Bear was sweating despite the breeze on his skin. Claustrophobia started to creep in despite the tall ceiling and the fact that the tunnel felt like it went on forever.

It was the darkness, pressing down on him like the hand of a giant.

The sound of voices floated toward them on the strange wind. Davis froze and the rest of the team followed, everyone gripping their weapons a little tighter. Bear could feel everyone's focus zero in on the blackness ahead of them. There was a soft glow to it, like there were lanterns lit in the distance.

When Davis was satisfied the voices weren't getting any closer, he motioned for the team to move forward. With short, quick steps, Bear stayed close to the woman in front of him, only looking behind him every few feet just to make sure there weren't going to be any surprises.

But sometimes you can't cheat fate.

A voice called out in Arabic. Bear recognized the warning, but it didn't matter. Within a matter of seconds all hell broke loose.

CHAPTER THIRTY-ONE

The scout must've been sitting stock-still in the darkness because no one saw him until he jumped up and ran off to the side, disappearing behind a row of concrete barriers and some rippling plastic. The sound triggered something in the back of Bear's mind, but he couldn't quite put his finger on it.

The team moved forward as one unit under Davis' direction, their footsteps in perfect unison. They were like a single creature with a dozen heads all on a swivel, weapons following the movements like many disjointed eyes. Bear briefly wondered if they looked like a demon coming to collect souls.

But the thought disappeared as soon as the first flash bang grenade was thrown. They didn't know how many people were in the other room, or how many of them were armed, but it was always better to be safe than sorry.

Davis called them forward as soon as the grenade went off. With everyone geared up from head to toe, the chance of a fatal shot was at a minimum, but the risk was still there. Bear and Sadie stayed on the other side of the barrier. Better to let the well-oiled machine clear out the room. He and Sadie could get the stragglers.

It was hard to see what was going on even ten feet in front of him. The flash bang grenade had caused the room to fill with smoke. That mixed with the soft yellow glow that had been barely fighting back the darkness meant visibility was at a minimum. The anti-terrorist unit was trained to clear a room like this, but it still seemed like a Herculean task. One wrong move and you could get turned around. And that meant you might shoot a team member instead of the enemy.

Grunts and screams filled the air, simultaneously full of fear and anger. The *pop, pop, pop* of the gunfire was mostly coming from the unit's side of the battle, but Bear could make out the volley of bullets. The men inside the room had been armed, but they hadn't been prepared for the onslaught they were being met with.

"Bear!"

Sadie's voice brought Bear out of his introspection about the battle in front of him. His head snapped in her direction, only to see her pointing her weapon directly at him. Instinct took over and he launched himself forward, down on his stomach, eating gravel, his beard saving him from scraping the skin from his chin.

A double *pop, pop* followed as soon as he was flat. Bear heard a grunt and a thud from behind him and twisted to see the body of a young man lying on the ground, an assault rifle in one hand. Blood was already forming a pool underneath him.

Bear turned back to Sadie. "Thanks."

"Any time," she said, but there was no lightness to her voice. It had been a close call.

"All clear," Davis called out. Then, presumably turning to a couple members of his team, "Pair up. Make sure the tunnel stays clear. We don't want any more surprises."

Bear and Sadie got to their feet and walked into the next room, their fingers flirting with trigger guards and their H&Ks pointed to the ground but still at the ready. Just because a room had been cleared didn't mean they were out of the woods yet. Anything could go wrong at any time.

It was a rough way to live your life, but it's what had kept Bear alive all this time.

"Define all clear," Bear said, spotting a pile of C-4 in the center of the room.

A woman from their team was kneeling at the base of the explosives. She looked up at Bear with green eyes so bright they shone through the darkness. "I wouldn't light a match or anything, but none of this is hooked up to any sort of timer or remote device. We're safe for now, but we need to move this out as soon as we can."

Bear nodded in understanding and looked around the room for the first time. It was long and narrow, lit by small construction lights that must've been abandoned along with the tunnel. The jihadists had white cloth over them to dull the brightness.

Aside from the pile of explosives, there was little else in the room. A chair here and there. A couple of blankets, like they had been living down here. A couple of cans of food, some opened some still sealed shut.

"They were holed up here for a while," Bear said, turning to Sadie. "They probably sent one or two guys up to the surface to get food every few days. Coming in and out of the tunnel would've been a risk. Someone was bound to spot them eventually."

"Yeah," Sadie said, but her voice was far away.

Bear followed her gaze and landed on a face he was surprised he recognized. It was Samson. He was on the ground, arms and legs splayed out to the side. A spray of bullets littered his body and a trickle of blood was still flowing from the corner of his mouth.

Bear didn't know what to say. Sadie hadn't been close with any of the agents, but they were still her men. They had been in London on her orders. And now at least two of them were dead. Whether or not they were your friends didn't matter. You take that kind of violence personally.

He'd noticed the corpses but had kept his eyes trained on what had been there before the showdown. Now he couldn't look past the men who had lost their lives today.

The first one he noticed was one of their own. He was the only one who fell during the confrontation, but there was a hush hovering over the entire team. One person dead was still one too many.

Bear didn't feel pity for the other men, the neo jihadists who had brought this upon themselves. But he didn't revel in the violence either. He wasn't like Miller, who enjoyed the thrill and the power that came with surviving when your enemy didn't.

As Bear looked around the room, he couldn't help but notice how young they all looked. They had to have been in their early 20s. Most were clean-shaven. Baby faces. Their lives couldn't have been easy to have led them here, but in death, they seemed so innocent. Like they couldn't have possibly wanted to plant a bomb in London's Underground in the hopes of destroying so many lives.

Bear didn't feel pity, but he did feel remorse. He had enlisted to help people. Everything he had chosen since leaving the Marines had been to help people. Sure, it was exciting and extravagant and sometimes even profitable, but at the end of the day it was about putting more good into the world than was being taken out of it.

And sometimes, like today, he wondered if he was really doing that.

Shouts from the other end of the room caught Bear's attention. He and Sadie moved in unison toward the group of agents who had gathered in a semicircle around something near the far wall. When the two of them got closer, Bear needed a few seconds to really understand what he was looking at.

It was Fredericks, bruised and bleeding but very much alive.

CHAPTER THIRTY-TWO

B ear could see the gamut of emotions running across Sadie's
face. Surprise. Relief. Confusion. Betrayal. Anger. It was
replaced by a mask of indifference and professionalism. This man
was a traitor, but he was still, at least for right now, a member of the
CIA. And they needed to know his side of the story.

Sadie pushed her way to the front of the group and Bear followed
in her wake.

"How is he?" she asked.

A young agent was kneeling beside him, a medical bag open at
Frederick's feet. "He's pretty beat up. They did a number on him
over the last week or so. Hasn't eaten in a while. Couple fractured
ribs. Several knife wounds to his upper thighs. A bullet wound in his
right shoulder. Nothing fatal."

"Is he in any immediate danger?" Sadie asked.

"Nah," the medic replied. "I stopped the bleeding. He'll be fine
to move. Once he gets to the hospital, we'll clean him up, get some
meds in him, and he should be good to go."

"I need to talk to him," Sadie said. She never took her eyes off
Fredericks. "Alone."

The medic looked up at Davis, who nodded. "Move out, ladies and gents. Give them some space."

As the crowd dispersed, Bear stood awkwardly to the side. Sadie shot him a look.

"If you need a minute," he started.

"Don't be an idiot," Sadie said. "Besides, I need someone to keep me from killing this asshole myself."

Bear laughed. Sadie hadn't bothered to keep her voice low. Fredericks clenched his jaw but Bear could tell there wasn't anger there. Shame, maybe. He knew he had fucked up.

"Who're you?" Fredericks asked, looking at Bear.

"One of the people who's been trying to save your sorry ass," Bear said.

Fredericks finally turned to Sadie. "I'm sorry—"

She held up a hand. "I don't want apologies. This is it for you. It's over. You're out. The only thing you can do now is tell us exactly what happened and why. Maybe you'll walk away from this without the word *traitor* attached to your name, but I honestly doubt it."

Fredericks swallowed audibly. "It was never supposed to go like this."

Sadie squatted down in front of him. That mask of indifference was still on her face, but Bear could see the anger and the pain just beneath the surface. "You mean you were never supposed to get caught."

Fredericks shook his head, then clutched his ribs. "It was never supposed to go this far. We were supposed to get paid and then take out the terrorists, no harm, no foul."

"That was a pretty big risk," Bear said. "You had no idea it wasn't going to blow up in your face. Literally."

"We had plans in place," Fredericks said. "Backups. Guarantees. But that all went to shit when they got wind of the double deal. They grabbed us, brought us down here where they tortured us. They killed Sheehan pretty much right away. Then they took a video of me and Samson. I'm gonna assume you saw that one already."

Bear looked around, taking in the plastic and the lights and the walls for what felt like the first time. This was where they'd shot the video Winters had shown them. The rustling was because of the plastic. The echo was because of the tunnel.

Bear briefly wondered if Samson and the other fallen agent would still be alive had he been able to put two and two together sooner.

"None of that lets you off the hook," Sadie said.

"I'm not trying to get off the hook," Fredericks said. "I know what I did. But you gotta believe me. I didn't want to do this."

Bear looked down at him. "That's not what we heard. Story goes that you're a greedy little bastard. Decided to be an entrepreneur. You wanted to make a nice comfy living off of cons like this."

Fredericks laughed, then clutched his side in pain. "Who told you that? It was probably Miller, wasn't it? That guy isn't right. Don't trust anything he tells you. He's smarter than he looks."

"So are you," Bear said. "So why should we trust you?"

"I've got proof," Fredericks said. "Back in the apartment. I can prove this wasn't my idea."

Bear was about to tell him his proof had gone up in smoke, but Sadie cut him off. "I'm willing to give you the benefit of the doubt here, but you're gonna have to give me something to go off of."

"There's a man named Thorne. CIA. One of the best. He's got a way of convincing people to do his dirty work. He doesn't like being told no."

Bear and Sadie exchanged a look.

"You know who he is, don't you?" Fredericks asked. He sighed and shifted and groaned until he got comfortable again. "That's why you're here."

"What did Thorne have on you?"

Fredericks took a moment to find his words. "I'll admit I'm not the best guy. And yeah, I can be a little greedy at times. Who doesn't want more money? To live more comfortably? We get sent to shitholes where we're expected to sleep in the mud or the snow or the desert. When I come home, I want the best of the best."

"So, you found a way to take a little off the top," Bear said.

Fredericks nodded. "It wasn't a lot. I made sure I never took anything that mattered. Not drugs or weapons or anything like that. Just stuff here and there that wouldn't be missed. Adjusted some numbers. Found a way to cut corners. Brought a few people in on the scheme. Trusted the wrong person."

"Who?" Sadie asked.

"Miller." Fredericks looked up at the ceiling and shook his head. "Should've known better."

"So you knew him before now?" Bear asked. "That's not the story he told us."

"He's a habitual liar. If you believe one thing I say today, it's that." Fredericks took a deep breath that appeared to be pretty painful. "He was a loose cannon back then. Still is, as a matter of fact. But I also knew he'd keep his mouth shut. At least to our CO."

"But?" Sadie pressed.

"But then he said something to Thorne. Didn't know who he was back then. Some spook who wanted to expand my operation. I got scared. Said no. Went cold turkey right then and there."

"You stopped skimming off the top?" Bear asked.

"Cold turkey," Fredericks repeated. "I didn't want any trouble. I wasn't looking to become some billionaire hotshot. I just wanted a nice house. A nice car. A couple luxuries. I liked traveling the world, meeting new people. Helping them. I didn't want out of that. What Thorne offered didn't interest me."

"I bet he took that nicely," Bear said.

"At the time? Yeah. He just said okay and moved on. I shut up shop and that was that. Miller tried to nudge me a couple times after that, but I just told him I'd gotten everything I'd needed. He got kicked out soon after that. I thought I was done with the whole thing."

Sadie stood up to stretch her legs. "But?"

"But he reached out again about a month ago. He was a little more convincing this time. Had evidence of every single thing I'd skimmed from the top while I was back in the Marines. Had information on my family. My sister and her kid. Said he needed a favor. I couldn't exactly say no."

Bear wanted to blame the guy for everything that had gone down since the three of them had gone missing, but once again it came down to Thorne. It always led back to Thorne.

"Why did Thorne want you to get mixed up in all of this?"

"Not a clue." When Bear and Sadie both looked at him with skepticism in their eyes, he tried sitting up and leaning forward. "No, really. I have no idea. I told him I'd do this and that'd be it. He seemed okay with that."

Sadie turned to Bear. "That's not like Thorne. Once he digs his claws into someone, he doesn't let them go."

"Unless they don't serve a purpose for him anymore," Bear said. "Maybe this wasn't about Fredericks and getting him on the roster. It was about the job."

Sadie returned her scrutinizing gaze back to Fredericks. "You really have no idea why this job was so important?"

"He didn't tell me much. I was supposed to get money from both the Irish gang and the neo jihadists, then shut down the cell and save the day. *Be the hero,* he said."

"He wanted a win for the CIA," Bear said. He could feel the pieces coming together, but they weren't quite locked in place yet.

Sadie looked at Bear. "No, he wanted a win for himself."

CHAPTER THIRTY-THREE

Sadie paced the room in a random and chaotic pattern. "Miller played us. Hard. He told us Thorne had no idea this job was even going on, but made sure to drop his name after minimal pressure. We thought it was to help himself, but if he's in as deep with Thorne as I think, he's only interested is keeping Thorne's name out of the dirt."

"So how does all of this help him?" Bear asked, gesturing around the room. "If Miller was so quick to name Thorne, that means Thorne wanted us to know he was behind this. How the hell does that benefit him?"

"If things had gone off without a hitch? The CIA would've been the good guys and Thorne could've swooped in to save the day. There'd be evidence that he set up the operation himself, scrubbing a few facts here and there like taking a little money on the side while they did that."

"What's the point, though?" Bear asked. "The CIA wouldn't let him out of his jail cell based on this alone."

"You know Thorne's got a dozen other jobs like this going on right now, right under our noses. He wants the CIA to recognize his genius. He wants to be in charge of keeping the peace. Right now, they think he's a loose cannon, but if he can pull all this off? They'd set him up in the Director's chair."

"He doesn't need that much power. Look what he can do on a shoestring budget," Bear said. "If he had the entire CIA backing him up? He wouldn't stop at world peace. He'd put a monopoly on war."

"I have documents," Fredericks said. "Proof that Thorne orchestrated this. Just let me get back to my apartment. I can give you everything you need to keep him locked away for good."

Bear looked at Sadie for permission before he let the news drop. "Hate to say it, pal, but your apartment went up in flames. Everything's gone."

All the color drained out of Fredericks' face. "Shit. Tell me you found something. Anything."

"Nothing," Sadie said. "Did you have backups? Is there anyone else who could corroborate with you?"

"No one willing to betray Thorne." Fredericks looked sicker than a few moments before. "Only me, Miller, and Noble knew the truth. And they aren't going to say a damn thing."

Bear felt like he'd been electrocuted. He froze, all his limbs tingling. The top of his head felt like it was on fire. Tunnel vision set in. A ringing in his ears. He could feel every nerve ending in his body, but he also saw himself from the outside, as if from above.

And that's why, even though his brain was telling him to stop, he couldn't keep himself from launching forward, grabbing Fredericks by the collar, and shouting, "What did you say?" over and over again in his face.

Sadie tried to pull him off Fredericks, but he had a death grip on the guy's tattered shirt.

Bear saw red. It was only when he realized his hands had moved from Fredericks' collar to his throat that Bear finally let go. The other man choked and sputtered while he regained his breath. Bear let Sadie pull him away, but he stopped when he was just out of arm's reach.

"Noble," Bear said. He could only get out one word at a time. "Everything. Now."

Fredericks' eyes were wild as they bounced from Sadie to Bear. He was obviously terrified, but he apparently didn't want to give Bear another reason to attack him. "I only met him once. Couldn't get a read on him. He came in with Miller one day. He was our backup plan, I guess. If everything went to shit, he'd clean it up. I didn't have to ask what that meant. I did everything to make sure I wasn't going to find out firsthand, either. And now..."

Bear's muscles were on fire as he kept himself from launching at Fredericks again. Sadie had to put her whole weight into pushing him a few feet further back.

"What's wrong with you?" she snapped. "Get your head together."

"Jack would never. With Thorne? Never." Bear was still having trouble forming whole sentences.

"I know that and you know that," Sadie said. She still held a firm hand on his chest, but her voice was softer now. "We both know this isn't what it looks like."

"Then what is it?" Bear said, finally finding something resembling composure. "Because I'm at the end of my rope, Sadie, and I'd really like some goddamn answers."

"So would I." When Sadie was sure Bear wasn't going to run forward again, she removed her hand from his chest and started pacing again. "Jack wouldn't be working with Thorne unless it was his only option. We both know that."

Bear could only grunt in assent.

"He's either trying to protect someone, or he must know what Thorne's master plan is. Maybe the only way he could stop it was by working with Thorne."

"As a fixer?" Bear asked. "We've done some shitty things in our past, he and I, but we always tried to keep our hands as clean as possible. This isn't clean, Sadie. To fix this, he'd have to shed a lot of blood. And some of that was bound to be innocent."

"We don't know that," Sadie said. "We don't have all the details yet."

Bear started looking around him wildly, barely taking in the fact that Davis and all the other agents were watching every move they made. "Jack must be close. He'd have to monitor this situation. He's probably been here all along. That means he knew what we were up to. He knew we were close. And he didn't help. He didn't come forward."

"We don't know why," Sadie said, more and more insistent. "There could be a million reasons—"

"I'm sorry," Fredericks said. His voice was low, but Sadie and Bear whipped their heads in his direction. He had slumped to the side, one arm in his lap and the other placed awkwardly behind his back. "This was never part of the plan."

"What was?" Sadie asked. She was creeping forward as slowly as she could. "What was never part of the plan?"

"I didn't want anyone to get hurt," Fredericks said. "But if there's no proof, Thorne won't even hesitate. My family is as good as dead."

"We can figure this out together," Sadie said. "There's still plenty we can do."

"There's only one thing to do," Fredericks said.

He didn't finish his thought. Instead, Fredericks pulled a pistol from behind his back and aimed it forward. Not at Bear. Not at Sadie. Not at anyone else standing in the room.

Instead, he aimed for the pile of C4 just over Bear's shoulder. It was enough to kill them all and level several city blocks above them.

Bear didn't think. He just moved. He dove in front of the explosives just as Fredericks pulled the trigger, cringing and apologizing as he did it.

Someone put a bullet in Fredericks' forehead, but he still got off two of his own shots.

Bear hit the ground having just felt a pair of bullets slam into his chest.

CHAPTER THIRTY-FOUR

"You're the reason why I'm getting gray hairs," Sadie said. "Not this job."

"You knew I was wearing a vest." Bear winced as he rubbed the darkening bruises on his chest.

"Knowing and remembering are two different things when your world is about to explode." Sadie paused for dramatic effect. "Literally."

"Yeah, yeah, I'm fine."

And he was. Bear had remembered he was wearing a vest when he dove in front of Fredericks' bullets. The only thing he had been worried about was timing his jump correctly. Anything other than perfect would've led to a bullet in his brain or something much worse.

That's not to say he was feeling his best. He was still banged up from when he had been jumped by the jihadists who had crawled out of the tunnel long enough to track him down. Stitches in his chest had opened up. Couple that with the two sizable bruises spreading across his skin, and Bear could honestly say he'd been better.

But all of that paled in comparison to what Fredericks had revealed to them.

Bear was still trying to process it. Still trying to piece it all together.

Jack had been mixed up in all of this, somehow.

Jack Noble. His friend. His brother.

He had known about the terrorist attack. Had let it get as far as it did. He had been hired by Thorne to clean up the mess if it had all gone sideways. He had watched and waited and had nearly let Bear get killed.

But Bear wasn't angry. Not at Jack, at least.

He was pissed at Fredericks, that was for sure. The man was a coward. He had been willing to kill thousands of innocent people just so he didn't have to face the consequences of his actions. When Bear had brought this up to Sadie, she had given him a noncommittal shrug.

"Maybe he was protecting his family," she had said. "We just don't know yet."

There were a lot of things they didn't know yet. But they were about to find out.

Sadie and Bear had two options. They could either stay in London and keep looking for Jack, or they could go back home and finally talk to Thorne face-to-face.

Sadie had made her decision on the spot. She needed to go to Langley to deal with the fallout of three of her agents losing their lives on the job. There was gonna be a lot of paperwork and a lot of explaining to do. Better to get it done sooner rather than later.

Bear, on the other hand, had been torn. He needed to talk to Jack.

Noble felt so close, like Bear would turn a corner and he'd be right there, waiting for him. Waiting to explain what the hell was going on and why he had teamed up with Thorne.

But the universe wasn't ready to spill her secrets just yet.

Without knowing where in the world Jack Noble was, Bear decided to follow Sadie home. Thorne was their best chance at getting some more answers, and unless Jack wanted to be found, no one would be able to lay a hand on him. Not even Bear.

So it was with that consideration Bear found himself waiting to board a plane back to Virginia. They were at Mr. Corbyn's airfield, as neither Sadie nor Bear had felt like dealing with public transportation that day. They'd take a private jet home instead.

It wasn't just for rich people and criminals, after all.

Mr. Corbyn shook their hands and thanked them for their service. Bear knew he meant well, but at the moment it just felt like rubbing salt in the wound. Sure, they'd stopped the terrorist attack, but all three missing agents were dead. And Jack was still missing. Had it really been worth it?

Bear knew it had, just to keep the bomb from exploding. But he couldn't help wishing he'd stayed home and just waited for Jack to reach out to him, eventually. They could've shared some great stories and a good laugh over a couple of beers and everything would be normal.

Director Winters had been waiting for them when they arrived.

Bear couldn't hold in his surprise as he shook her hand. "Is it normal for the Director of MI5 to see a couple Americans off as they fly back home?"

Winters laughed. "Not really, but you did us a great service today. Not only did you stop a terrorist attack from happening, but you discovered a new faction, something for us all to keep an eye on. Your country will be proud of you. I know I am."

"Thank you," Sadie said. She paused, looking around. "Where's Maria?"

"I sent her home ahead of you. I wasn't sure how long you would be and Langley was quite interested in their own line of questioning for the young woman."

"We appreciate you giving us space to carry out our mission. And letting us in on the op to take down the cell."

"I recognize a good agent when I see one," Winters said, looking at Sadie. Then she switched to Bear. "And whatever you are, Mr. Logan, you're a good one, too."

He couldn't stop the laugh that erupted from his mouth. "Thanks. That's a pretty high compliment coming from you."

"It is." There was a twinkle in Winters' eye. "Don't get used to it."

"I used to love London," Bear said, wistfully. "But I wouldn't be too upset if I didn't cross your path again anytime soon, Director."

Winters' smile fell, but she looked like she understood. "There are a few cities like that on the map for me, too. London, thankfully, will always be my home. No matter how turbulent the waters get."

Bear nodded. He knew what that felt like. That was New York for him.

"I hope you find what you're looking for," Winters said, holding out her hand to him.

Bear hesitated. "What do you mean?"

"You seem lost, Mr. Logan. From the day you set foot at MI5, you've seemed disconnected. Whatever it is you've been searching for, I hope you come across it soon. There's nothing worse than finding yourself floating, detached from the rest of the world. Especially for people like us."

Bear shook her hand, but the comment still didn't sit right with him. Did she know about Jack, or was she really that observant? A lot of people in this line of work knew how to read between the lines, whether that was body language or all the stuff you didn't say. Winters was a smart woman, Bear knew that for sure, but Dottie had warned him that she also liked keeping the whole truth close to her chest.

And Director Winters had proven she was smart. Dottie was good at her job—one of the best, if Bear was being honest—but that didn't mean she was infallible. Had Director Winters overheard either one of their conversations? It was more than just a little possible.

If that was the case, it was now a question of whether or not

Winters was hiding something. Maybe she knew exactly where Noble was—or knew someone who did—and didn't want to divulge that information. Was it because she had something to hide or because she didn't want to stick her nose in someone else's business? Sometimes it was better to keep your hands clean.

"And I hope they don't give you too much trouble back home," Winters continued, shaking Sadie's hand. She didn't notice the strange look on Bear's face.

"Thanks," Sadie said, returning the gesture. "I'll be all right."

Winters checked her watch and started walking away. "I've got to go. Have a safe trip home. I hope to see you both again under better circumstances."

Sadie stopped her. "What about the prisoners? Were they freed?"

Winters turned and let a smile slip past. "Fortunately we had the foresight to keep them in holding until we heard from the cell again. During that time, some of the best interrogators went to work on the men and it was determined they had absolutely no connection with the terrorists. It was all a diversion meant to buy some time."

Bear joined Sadie in a chuckle and wondered if he'd ever really find the story amusing.

Winters turned again and set off.

Sadie waved, but Bear just kept staring after her like if he did it hard enough, he'd be able to read her mind.

"What's wrong?" Sadie asked.

"Think she knows anything about Jack?"

Sadie put her arm down and turned to him. "Why would she know anything about Jack?"

"She's the Director of MI5. I imagine not a lot escapes her notice."

Sadie was silent for a minute. "I want to find him too, Bear, but—"

"Thorne is the priority now." Bear started walking toward the plane. "Yeah, I know."

Sadie and Bear loaded onto the plane, saying hello to their

captain in the process. The trip should be slightly shorter than on a commercial flight. Bear was grateful for that. After everything he'd been through, the last thing he wanted to do was spend any more time on a plane than absolutely necessary.

Sadie's phone buzzed just as Bear was making sure his seatbelt was nice and tight. He didn't have the cocktail of drugs at his disposal that he'd had when he first came over, and he was already regretting everything about this flight. Smaller planes meant more turbulence. He didn't care how fancy a private jet was. They could never avoid the turbulence.

Sadie hung up the phone and turned to Bear. Her face was a mask of confusion and anger.

"What's wrong?" he asked.

"Maria slipped her detail," she said. "She's missing."

CHAPTER THIRTY-FIVE

"They're just going to let me walk in there with you and talk to Thorne?" Bear asked. "Seems convenient."

Sadie laughed. "While you were passed out on the plane, I spent eight hours convincing my superiors to let you interrogate him with me. There was nothing convenient about it."

Private jets apparently came with expensive bottles of whiskey, which meant Bear drank as many as it would take to knock him out on the trip back home. It resulted in some pretty restless sleep and more than one crazy dream—not to mention the hangover—but it got the job done. Bear didn't remember the plane ride.

"And how exactly did you convince them?"

Sadie blew a piece of hair out of her eyes. "You were there in Costa Rica and again in Korea. You're a pivotal part of this investigation and of particular interest to Thorne. Plus, with Jack missing, I told them it was best to have the person who knows him best on board. It was a lot of phone calls and emails, but in the end, they knew it was the best call."

"For who?" Bear asked, under his breath. He looked up at the prison entrance that housed Thorne, waiting for the pair of them to be buzzed in.

He wanted to be here, sure. He wanted to look Thorne in the eyes and ask him what the hell was going on. But he also knew Thorne wasn't going to give up his answers easily. And any answers he did give would probably be part of the plan. They were playing right into Thorne's hand and they both knew it. But what other choice did they have?

"Any word on Maria?" Bear asked.

Sadie shook her head. "As soon as they landed back in Virginia, she gave her detail the slip. No one has seen or heard from her since."

"Who made up her detail?"

"Two of Winters' men. Apparently, they're just as pissed as we are."

"I doubt that."

Sadie looked at him from the corner of her eye. "What makes you say that?"

"I don't trust Winters."

"She's been more than forthcoming with us. She could've stopped us having damn near any involvement in everything that happened in London, but she didn't."

"That doesn't mean she wasn't still withholding information."

"Why does it sound like you know something I don't?" Sadie asked.

"I have a friend at MI5," Bear said. "Actually, she's a friend of Jack's."

"The one who knew Jack had been in London."

Bear grunted in assent. "She told me to be careful around Winters. Said she's a good person but that she plays things close to the chest. Winters might not go out of her way to make things more difficult for us, but that doesn't mean things won't get complicated if she's not telling us the whole truth."

"She was awfully helpful." When Bear shot her a look, Sadie

continued. "Have you ever met the head of a foreign intelligence agency that is willing to let us in on their operations?"

"That's the problem," Bear said. "It was too easy. Like she wanted to keep us close. Something else has gotta be going on here."

Sadie looked hesitant. "Look, I get being paranoid. And I'm not trying to convince you that you're wrong here."

"But?" Bear asked. He knew it was coming.

"It's nice to think someone is being straightforward for once."

"Well then we're in the wrong place," Bear said. "Don't hold your breath hoping to get a straight answer from Daniel Thorne."

"You're not wrong," Sadie said. "But I'm hoping we can trust Winters. It would be nice to have someone like that on our side."

Bear didn't say anything in return. Instead, he watched as a pair of guards finally met them at the prison entrance and silently checked their credentials. They took a little longer looking at Bear's visitor pass, but in the end, they waved both of them through.

The prison was high security, and Thorne was held in the most closely observed section. Sadie had explained that Thorne was a bit of a celebrity around here, both with the prisoners and the guards. He had a way of worming into a person's psyche. He had to be kept in isolation and his personal guards were switched out every few weeks so no one person was around him for too long.

The prison itself looked as high tech as they came, which didn't exactly sit well with Bear. Thorne was smart, and if there was a way to hack into the system, he'd find it. Or one of his many, many lackeys would. They needed to make sure there was a good old-fashioned bolt on the outside of Thorne's door just in case.

Bear filed away the note to bring it up later.

For now he followed the pair of guards down a series of hallways and through a number of gates that could only be opened when they both put their key cards against the digital readers. A loud buzz echoed around the hall each time, and the four of them moved in unison from one section of the prison to the next.

It took a solid fifteen minutes to make their way to the interrogation room where they'd be meeting Thorne. There would be no cameras and no mics inside. Even a piece of shit like Thorne had the right to meet in confidence with his lawyer, and this was the room he would be allowed to do that in.

But they weren't taking any chances. Two guards would be stationed outside the room in case Thorne decided to cause any trouble. Sadie had a recorder in her pocket, too. He probably wouldn't give anything away—he was too smart for that—but on the off chance he let something slip, she wanted to be able to play it back again and again.

Bear wasn't arguing. They were desperate now.

The two guards ahead of them stopped in front of a room with a solid steel door and no window. There was another dual digital lock here, but they didn't open it right away.

"You have half an hour," the man on the right said. He wore a hat that he kept low over his eyes. "We open the door after thirty minutes exactly, whether or not you're done."

"Understood," Sadie said.

"Do not underestimate him," the man said. He sounded tired, like he'd seen firsthand the kind of manipulation Thorne was capable of.

"We appreciate the warning," Sadie said. "But we know who we're dealing with."

Bear leaned forward, like he was sharing a particularly interesting secret. "We're kind of the ones that put him in here."

Bear could tell the man's eyebrows shot to the top of his head, even while they were hidden by his hat. "That doesn't make any sense."

Sadie folded her arms across her chest. "Why not?"

"He was *ecstatic* to get to see you."

"Trust me," Bear said, "that makes perfect sense."

The two guards exchanged looks but didn't say anything further. Instead, they stood in front of their respective lock, held out their key card, then looked at each other and nodded. After a countdown, they pressed their badge against the reader, and a loud buzz filled the air.

The man in the hat stepped to the side while the other guard pulled open the door and gestured for Bear and Sadie to walk through. After exchanging a look of their own, the two visitors entered the room one after the other, uncertain as to what exactly they'd be able to accomplish today.

Thorne sat at the table in the center of the room, his hands and feet chained down. He looked the same as ever, only without his usual flair for style. Still, Bear thought he made the orange jumpsuit work. His hair wasn't in disarray and he was still clean-shaven. The smile on his face seemed genuine. It made him look almost normal.

Thorne spread his arms as wide as the chains would allow them to go. "Bear. Sadie. You are both a sight for sore eyes."

CHAPTER THIRTY-SIX

"You're looking well," Sadie said. It didn't sound like she meant it as a compliment.

Bear kept his greeting to himself. It wouldn't have gone over very well.

"Working with what I have," Thorne replied. He ran a hand through his hair. "Everyone here is quite cordial despite the circumstances."

"Too bad," Bear said. He and Sadie sat across from the man who had caused them so much trouble over the last several months.

Thorne laughed. "Yes, I'm sure it would've been nice to see me roughed up a bit, huh, Riley?"

"You've still got plenty of time yet."

"I do, I do." Thorne didn't seem too concerned about it, though. "By the way, you can put that recorder in your pocket on the table, Sadie."

Sadie clenched her jaw but brought the recorder out, regardless.

"There is one issue, though." Thorne brought his own device.

"Is that an audio jammer?" Bear asked. "How did you get that?"

"Not easily," Thorne said, turning it on. "I have one or two friends around here. Even so, it's been mighty hard to hang on to. I'm glad you came when you did. Otherwise, we wouldn't be having a private conversation right now."

Bear didn't know how to answer that, and it seemed Sadie was at a loss for words, too.

"I think this is going to work best if we're both one hundred percent honest with each other, don't you?" Thorne asked.

Bear laughed. "Are you even capable of that?"

"Oh, yes. Especially when it benefits me."

"That sounds about right," Sadie looked at Bear. "You wanna go first?"

Bear leaned in. "Where to start?"

"Let's start with Jack," Thorne said. "How is he?"

Now it was Bear's turn to clench his jaw. "We haven't talked in a while."

Thorne's face fell. "That's unfortunate."

"Jack and I will be fine. You should be worrying about yourself."

"Oh, I am," Thorne said. "It would've been a lot easier if Jack could've explained his role in all of this. You don't exactly have a history of trusting me."

"And for good reason," Sadie pointed out.

Thorne waved the comment away. "Water under the bridge."

"For you, maybe."

There was a seriousness to Thorne that Bear hadn't seen before. He didn't necessarily look afraid, but for once he looked out of answers.

"Something not go according to plan?" Bear asked.

"You could say that." Thorne tugged on his sleeves like they were the cuffs on a dress shirt. "Can't say I'm too surprised."

Sadie slid her palms across the table. "Are you going to start making sense anytime soon?"

Thorne looked around the room like he was searching for hidden cameras. "If I tell you this, there's going to be a target on your back. A big one. To be honest, there probably already is. And if you run, you can't stop until you get to the end of this."

Bear was used to threats, but this felt heavier than that. Like a warning. Except it sounded like Thorne was trying to help them. Was he even capable of that?

Sadie must've felt the gravity of the situation, too. "I'm listening."

"We're gonna need to start at the beginning," Thorne said.

"London?" Bear asked.

Thorne shook his head. "Costa Rica."

Sadie stiffened. That place didn't hold good memories for any of them.

"Do you know why I wanted Goddard dead?" Thorne asked.

"The pipeline." Bear dragged the memory forward like it had been stuck in mud. "You had a stake in it."

Thorne rolled his eyes. "Too easy. No, that's not the reason. What about you, Sadie, do you have a guess?"

"Cut the bullshit and just tell us."

"You guys don't know how to have any fun." Thorne sat up a little straighter and folded his hands in front of him. "He was a traitor."

Bear and Sadie remained silent. Bear, at least, wasn't going to believe a word Thorne said without some evidence. But he was at least going to listen.

"Senator Goddard was collecting secrets and selling them to the highest bidder. The pipeline was just the tip of the iceberg. He was blackmailing half of congress into making sure the deal went through, but that was only his day job. At night, he was selling national secrets to foreign powers."

"And you were the guy sent in to take him out?" Bear asked. "Seems a little below your pay grade."

"It's not," Thorne said, shooting him a withering look. "But no. My job was to monitor the good senator. Collect evidence. See what he was really doing in his spare time. To be honest, most people knew about his hobby. He wasn't exactly keeping a low profile. There's a reason why he went into politics instead of the CIA."

"If everyone knew about it," Sadie said, "then why didn't anyone take care of the issue before?"

"Believe it or not, he was helping us." When Sadie and Bear gave him a blank stare, he continued. "Those who knew about his little side job made it a point to keep tabs on where the information was going once it left his hands. We'd find out someone was interested, we'd track them down, and then take out the threat before they ever had a chance to make use of the intel."

"And no one got suspicious?" Sadie asked.

"No one important. Certainly not Goddard. Sometimes we'd let little bits of information go free. Nothing too devastating. Just so he could keep his reputation as a solid informant."

"People got hurt, didn't they?" Sadie asked. "When you let the information fall into the wrong hands."

Thorne shrugged. "It was necessary to the overall cause."

Sadie banged her fist on the table. "We're supposed to protect people."

"And we are," Thorne said. "Sometimes sacrifices need to be made. I'd love to live in your idyllic little world, Sadie, but it's not realistic. I don't like it any more than you do."

"Are you sure about that?" Bear asked.

"I'm an asshole," Thorne said. "Not a psychopath."

Bear snorted. "That's to be determined."

"Are you going to continue insulting me or do you want to hear the rest of what I have to say?"

"I'm not making any promises."

Thorne shot him a look, but didn't argue. "Goddard was a good asset until he wasn't. He got his hands on the wrong information."

"Korea," Sadie supplied. "He found out about the government's hand in North Korea's current regime."

Thorne nodded sagely, like Sadie was his star pupil. "Correct. After Goddard's death, we had some cleaning up to do."

"You keep saying *we*," Bear interjected. "Who?"

"Quite a few people and organizations. Your friend Frank, for one."

"He's not my friend."

Thorne ignored Bear. "The CIA, for another. But there are others."

"You had cleaning up to do," Sadie said, shooting Bear a look that told him she didn't like that Thorne had gotten off track. "How?"

"The usual methods. For those he was blackmailing, we let some off the hook. For others, Goddard was simply replaced by someone else. As for the people he leaked information to, I made it a point to pay them all a little visit. Some were taken out, while others were allowed to live—for a price."

"And Korea?" Sadie asked.

"Korea was more complicated." Thorne's voice was almost wistful, like he had enjoyed the challenge. "We had to track the information Goddard had sold, then figure out the best way to infiltrate the government and take care of the problem."

"And you figured the best way was us?" Bear asked.

"You had impressed me in Costa Rica," Thorne said, with a shrug. "I wanted to know what you were both capable of and see how long I could keep my hands clean of the situation."

"Then we threw you a curveball," Sadie said.

"*You* threw me a curveball," Thorne said. His voice was a little tighter now. "It was a good one, too. Unfortunate for us all, but impressive nonetheless. Your resume is on a lot more desks these days. I wouldn't be surprised if a promotion was in the near future for you. If there's a future for us at all, that is."

Sadie scoffed, but Bear cut her off. "Why is it unfortunate for us all?"

"Because now I'm exactly where they want me."

"Who?" Sadie asked.

"You wouldn't believe me if I told you." When Bear tried to

argue, Thorne held up his hand—at least as far as the chain would allow him to. "That's where Jack was supposed to come in."

Now it was Sadie's turn to cut off Bear. "One thing at a time. First, why is it unfortunate you're in here? I feel a lot safer at night."

"You shouldn't," Thorne said. His face had transformed back into the serious, almost-scared version of itself. "I was your last line of defense."

"Stop being cryptic," Bear said. "You wanted to spill your guts, so spill them. Our time is running out."

"That it is." Thorne closed his eyes and took a deep breath. When he opened them again, it looked like he had re-centered himself. His voice was calm and neutral. Any fear that had been dancing around the surface of his face was gone. "Goddard had a lot of secrets in his back pocket. Like I said, most of them were pretty harmless. One was not."

"Korea?" Bear asked.

"Worse than that." Thorne tried to put his hands in his lap, was stopped by the chain, and put them back on top of the table. "We found out that someone very prominent, someone the average person would know by name, was putting pieces into place that would cause wholesale destruction the likes of which the world has never seen before."

"That sounds dramatic," Bear said. "And Goddard was just sitting on this information?"

"Of course not." Thorne sounded offended now. "He was an idiot. He had all the puzzle pieces, but he didn't even think to put them together. I did."

"Lucky for us," Bear said.

"Lucky for everyone," Thorne said. He leaned forward, his face serious again. "I'm not kidding, Riley. I'm not putting on theatrics. We're talking about the start of World War III. This has been in the works for some time now. The dominoes have been set up. All they need is a good push. That's what I've been trying to prevent. That's what you stopped me from doing when you threw me in here."

"Then why are you even in here?" Sadie asked. "If all this was in service to the United States, why are you still locked up?"

"Haven't you been listening?" Thorne looked like he was losing it for the first time since they stepped foot in the room. "I'm right where they want me. They're not going to let me out now. Not until everything is set in motion."

"You always have a backup plan," Bear said. "So what is it this time?"

Thorne looked directly at Bear when he said the one thing Bear was hoping he wouldn't.

"Jack."

CHAPTER THIRTY-SEVEN

"How in the hell did you ever get Jack in on this?" Bear asked. "He hates you more than I do."

Thorne laughed. "You're not wrong. But once I showed him the evidence, he was on board. Didn't have much of a choice."

"Why not?" Sadie asked.

"Wholesale destruction, remember?" Bear said. "The likes of which—"

"You're not going to be laughing much longer," Thorne said. "Trust me."

"That I'll never do," Bear said, leaning forward. "And you sound like some crazy tin-hat."

"You know better than to believe all conspiracy theories are bullshit. There's truth in all of them—some more than others."

"We don't have time for your witty banter," Sadie said, glaring between both Bear and Thorne. "Tell us how this ties in with what happened in London."

"London was the first domino," Thorne said. "There are a series of attacks planned, all around the world, and London was supposed to be the first."

"You knew about it and you didn't do anything to stop it," Sadie said.

"Wrong." Thorne shifted in his seat. "That's what Jack was for."

"What about Maria?" Sadie asked. "How does she play into all of this?"

Thorne's features softened ever so slightly. "How is she?"

"Do you care?" Bear asked. "I put a gun to her head and you practically begged me to pull the trigger."

"I never wanted her to get hurt."

"Does she know about all this?" Sadie asked.

"Bits and pieces," Thorne said. "Not the big picture. She wasn't ready for that."

"She's in the wind," Bear said. "I'm guessing there's a target on her back, too?"

"Most likely," Thorne said. "But she's smart. She'll be able to survive on her own."

Sadie shook her head, but there was nothing they could do for Maria now. "What about Fredericks?"

"What about him?" Thorne said. "He's a useful idiot."

"A dead idiot."

Thorne's eyes cut to Sadie, and then to Bear. "That's unfortunate."

"He nearly set the bomb off himself," Sadie said. "Luckily, Bear stopped him."

"Like I said, he's an idiot," Thorne said.

"Was," Bear corrected.

"Regardless," Thorne said. "The idea was to flush out whoever is behind this."

"Did it work?"

"No, but it was a long shot."

"You tried anyway," Sadie said. Her voice got louder with each word. "Despite the risk."

"Yes." Thorne shifted in his seat and for the first time he looked desperate. "This is worth the risk. It's worth every risk. This person—"

"Who you won't name," Bear interjected.

"—is smart." Thorne glared at him. "They won't be caught red-handed. But that doesn't mean we shouldn't try."

"You know about the other attacks," Sadie said. "Why not tell someone?"

"You're not listening to me," Thorne said, banging his fists on the table. "There's no one to tell. The people I would tell are probably in on it."

"For what purpose?" Sadie asked.

Thorne tried to throw his hands up and was stopped short by the shackles around his wrists. "Because war is profitable. And the United States needs a solid win to reestablish itself as the strongest nation in the world."

"You profit from war." Bear sat back in his chair and folded his arms across his chest. "Why are you trying to stop this one?"

Thorne closed his eyes. When he opened them again, it seemed like he had found a sense of calm. "Believe it or not, there are people I care about in this world. Not to mention my own life. World War III? That would make it a little difficult to maintain my current lifestyle."

Sadie checked her watch. She turned to Bear. "Time's almost up. Let's pretend we believe him for the next three minutes."

Bear shrugged but didn't comment. He hated that Thorne seemed to be telling the truth, but he'd been burned before. "Fine. What's the next step?"

"Run," Thorne said. "And then link up with Jack."

"Where is he?"

"I don't know. I assume he'll get in contact with you if he thinks it's safe. He'll prove that what I'm saying is true."

"And then what?" Sadie asked. "We save the world?"

"Do you have another option?" Thorne asked.

"Why Jack?" Bear asked.

Thorne shrugged. "Why not? He's an independent entity. He's

practically invisible. Can come and go as he pleases. No one would be watching him, and if they were, he'd be able to shake 'em easy enough."

"How did you know he wouldn't shoot you dead?"

"I didn't," Thorne said. "Almost came to that, too. You guys really hold a grudge."

"And for good reason," Sadie said.

"But Jack's a reasonable guy. Took some convincing, but in the end, he listened to what I had to say. I hope you will, too."

"And you're safe here?" Bear asked, looking around the room.

"Like I said, I'm right where they want me. They can keep an eye on me here. I'm their biggest threat."

"Then why aren't you dead?"

Thorne laughed. "Because I'm useful. They'll try to squeeze every ounce of information out of me. And then they'll probably try to pin this all on me, too."

"They were talking about that in London," Bear said. "Definitely made it look like you wanted to flatten the city."

"What I don't understand," Sadie said, "is why we're even talking right now? If Langley is in on this, they could've stopped me from coming here."

There was a cursory knock on the door. Thorne leaned forward. Sadie and Bear had to mirror him just to hear what he had to say.

"They'll want to know what we talked about. You're just another pawn to them. Trust no one. Never stop moving. Find out what's next and stop it. If you don't, you might as well say goodbye to everyone you know."

Bear didn't know what to say. He didn't want to believe it. It seemed crazy. World War III? Someone in their own government pulling strings all across the world to ensure a global war just to turn a profit? It was something that belonged on a website named theyare-outtogetus.com.

Then again, this was the world today. Global interdependence meant a slight tipping of the scale in the wrong direction could cause massive destruction. Bear had stopped a terrorist attack or two in his day. He knew how precarious the balance was.

The guard in the hat pushed open the door. "Time's up."

Sadie stood up. She looked down at Thorne, giving him no indication what she thought of everything he said. "Thank you for your time."

Thorne nodded his head as his gaze settled on the wall behind them.

The two guards led Sadie and Bear out of the room and down the hall. Bear wanted to talk to Sadie, to ask her what she thought about what Thorne said. She seemed calmer than he felt, but that didn't mean she wasn't struggling with everything he had divulged to them.

Bear shook himself free of the doubt in his head. He knew what he needed to do next.

Find Jack.

The two guards opened the door and ushered Bear and Sadie through. Once they were alone, Sadie shot Bear a look.

"What?!" he asked.

"What do you mean what? After all that, you've got nothing to say?"

"At the moment, no. It's a lot to take in."

"I believe him."

Bear stopped dead. "Seriously?"

Sadie kept walking. "A lot of it adds up. Something has felt off about all of this from the beginning. Even before I left for London there were little things here and there. I was getting pushback where I normally wouldn't. There were obstacles and delays. More than usual."

Bear didn't say anything.

"And if Jack is on board? That must've been some pretty convincing evidence."

"Thorne said Jack's on board," Bear reminded her. "We don't know that for sure."

"Fair enough." Sadie pushed her way through the final gate and headed toward her car. "How are we going to find him?"

"According to Thorne, he's going to find us," Bear said. "I just hope he does it sooner rather than later."

It was Sadie's turn to stop dead in her tracks. "Yeah, that might not be possible."

Bear followed her gaze across the parking lot, toward her car. Three black sedans were blocking her in. A pair of agents stood at the hood of one, talking to each other but keeping their eyes fixed on their targets. It was clear they were here for Bear and Sadie.

"Friends of yours?" Bear asked.

"Not exactly," Sadie said. She started moving again and Bear followed her lead. "But they're definitely CIA."

"What do you think they want?"

"To know about London," Sadie said. "But if what Thorne said is true, they want more than that."

"To keep us detained," Bear said.

"Exactly." Sadie spoke out of the corner of her mouth now. "Don't give them anything of consequence."

"Copy that," Bear said.

Sadie strolled forward, holding out her hand to the agent closest to her. "How can I help you, boys?"

CHAPTER THIRTY-EIGHT

B ear had been at Langley for close to six hours now. He was tired, hungry, and done with the entire situation. But he couldn't tell them that. Couldn't show it, either. They were looking for anything to latch on to, and he was doing his best to avoid giving them any footholds. He knew once they grabbed on, they'd never let go.

The car ride to Langley had been congenial, if not a little awkward. Everyone knew what was happening, but no one would admit it. Bear and Sadie had become persons of interest thanks to their little chat with Thorne. The CIA was probably looking forward to hearing what secrets Thorne was going to spill, but the second he turned on that audio scrambler, the gloves had to come off.

Then again, if what Thorne was saying was true, Bear and Sadie had become persons of interest well before visiting the prison that morning. They'd been under surveillance since London. Maybe even earlier. Maybe even since Costa Rica.

As soon as they had shaken hands with the agents, Sadie and Bear had been ushered into two separate cars. He wasn't worried, though. Despite the various ups and downs during this trip, he trusted her. Neither one of them would throw the other under the bus, and they'd do the best they could to protect Jack if he came up in the conversation.

So far he hadn't.

Instead, Bear had to go through their mission in London, starting with the second he landed, and walk the two agents across from him through every moment since. He talked about Mr. Jones, the apartment building, the kid, the fire, the safe house, MI5 headquarters, and then the mess that continued from there on out. He ended with the close call in the tunnel. The fact that Fredericks had been dirty and that all three agents were now dead.

Then they started asking about Sadie. What did Bear think of her? Was she a good leader? Trustworthy? Did he think she had been in on the scheme? Was her lack of judgment due to inexperience or something else? Did he think she shouldn't have gone back into the field so quickly?

It was at this point that Bear couldn't help himself. "She caught Thorne, didn't she? Better than you guys could do. Better than I could do. None of this is her fault. Without her, we all would've been fucked."

But Bear had said the magic word. Thorne. The conversation took such a sharp turn, he nearly got whiplash.

The two agents across from him were exactly who you'd think would work at the CIA. They were in their fifties, with graying hair and sharp, beady eyes. They both wore black suits and ties with a crisp white shirt on underneath. The one on the right, Peterson, had a silver mustache that glinted in the light if he turned just so. The one on the left, LaSalle, had one milky eye.

Bear desperately wanted to know what had happened to him.

"What made you want to talk to Thorne?" LaSalle asked. He had a deep, gravelly voice like Tom Selleck.

"Sadie wanted me there. Said she spent eight hours clearing it with you guys."

LaSalle neither confirmed nor denied that statement. "What did you talk about?"

They had spent six hours making sure Bear was mentally exhausted before asking the question they really wanted to know the answer to. But Bear had been ready for this since the beginning. He'd made his decision on the car ride over. And just like Sadie, he was going to make sure he didn't give them anything of consequence.

But they also weren't going to believe anything less than the truth.

"He tried to convince us that he was innocent. That there was some insane global conspiracy and he was the only good guy on the roster."

LaSalle and Peterson exchanged a look.

Bear laughed. "You have the same look Sadie and I had on our faces. Dude is crazy."

"You didn't believe him?" LaSalle asked. Peterson remained silent and stoic, but raised a single eyebrow like he was adding his own question mark to the end of his partner's inquiry.

"Hell no." Bear stopped laughing. He had to sell it. "Are you kidding me? I spent months tracking this guy down. He's smart and he's crazy. If there's a conspiracy at all, chances are he's the one in the middle of it."

"What if he's telling the truth?"

Bear shrugged. "Not my problem. That's on you guys. I don't work for you."

"That could change," LaSalle started.

Bear held up a hand. "No, thank you. I'm getting too old for this shit. I have too much excitement in my life as it is."

Peterson spoke up for what was probably the third or fourth time in the last six hours. "What about Jack Noble?"

Bear couldn't help his reaction. He turned his head sharply to look at Peterson. "What about him?"

"We have reason to believe he's working with Thorne," LaSalle said.

"Never." Bear was adamant. "Never. He hates Thorne more than I do. If Jack ever saw him, he'd probably put a gun to his head."

"And kill an agent of the CIA?" LaSalle asked.

"You don't think Thorne deserves that and worse? He's been a pain in your ass, too."

Neither of the men across from Bear could exactly deny that.

"And before you ask," Bear continued, "the answer is no."

"No?"

"I don't know where Jack is. Haven't heard from him in months."

"Is that unusual?" LaSalle asked. He flipped open a file folder and rifled through the pages like he had Jack's and Bear's entire friendship in black and white right in front of him. He probably did. "You two seem close."

"It's been known to happen before," Bear said. "We check in when we can. Lay low when we can't. Thorne proved he wasn't worth the trouble, so both Jack and I decided to take an extended vacation."

"And yet here you are," LaSalle said.

"Because of Thorne." Bear tried to keep his annoyance in check, but it was getting harder and harder. "Guess I was easier to find than Jack."

"We have reason to believe Jack was in London at the same time you were."

"If he was, I never saw him."

"Did you know he was there?"

Bear hesitated for a split-second. They may know about the conversation he had with Dottie. If he lied and they called him out on it, everything he had said previously would be put into question. If he told the truth, they may hold him even longer just to get a few more nuggets of information out of him. Neither option was enticing.

Bear went with his gut.

"No," Bear said. "I had no idea. If I had, I would've stuck around. Tried to find him."

"Do you think you would've been able to?" LaSalle asked. "Find him, I mean."

Bear blew out a big breath. They'd believed the lie. "Doubtful. I'd mostly be walking in circles waiting for him to show his ass."

LaSalle and Peterson exchanged another look, but when Peterson didn't have any further questions, LaSalle shuffled his files and folders together and folded his hands on top. "Daniel Thorne is considered a danger to this country and its allies. Without evidence that says otherwise, it's our belief that the same word of warning should be extended to Jack Noble."

"You think Jack's a terrorist?" Bear couldn't help but laugh. "After everything he's done?"

"Daniel Thorne was a hero once, too," Peterson said.

"Jack's not a bad guy," Bear said, knowing how weak his words sounded.

"We'd like to believe so," LaSalle said. "But we need to talk to him first."

"I don't know where he is," Bear said. "I already tried everything I know."

"We're aware." LaSalle stood up and motioned that Bear should do the same. "When he reaches out to you, we'll be prepared. It was good talking to you, Mr. Logan."

Bear shook both LaSalle and Peterson's hands, but the exchange wasn't a pleasant one. It had been a warning.

But it wasn't one that Bear had needed. As much as he believed Thorne was insane, he couldn't help but think the guy was telling the truth, especially after how quickly the CIA had come to collect both him and Sadie. Something was up, and even if the CIA wasn't explicitly in on it, they could be unknowingly working for whoever this person was that seemed to be pulling the strings.

Bear needed to talk to Jack sooner rather than later, but he had been honest when he said he had tried everything he knew. Now it was just a matter of time, waiting for Jack to finally emerge from the shadows and explain what the hell was going on here.

CHAPTER THIRTY-NINE

It had been six months since that day Bear was questioned by LaSalle and Peterson, and not a day went by that he didn't think about it. But that was all he had been allowed to do. He had only talked to Sadie once since then, and he certainly hadn't heard from Jack.

After he was released, he tried waiting around for Sadie, to see how she was and to hear what she had told them. But it had been obvious he was no longer welcome at Langley. A different pair of agents had ushered him into a car and driven him to the airport. He got on the next flight to New York.

Bear spent the next week laying low, not sure what would come at him. He was more than a little paranoid that whatever mess Thorne had dumped at his front door was about to kick it down. But everything was silent. Everything was still.

Until Sadie showed up one night.

She hadn't stayed long. He'd tried to offer her dinner, or at least a drink, but she was antsy. Paranoid, even. He'd never seen her look like that before. She kept parting his blinds to check the street, then positioning herself out of the line of sight of the windows.

She'd made him reassure her three times that he'd checked for bugs in his apartment. He had. Twice. It was clean. She didn't feel any better about that, and if he was being honest with himself, he didn't either. Thorne's paranoia was starting to get to him, and that was saying something. Bear was paranoid enough as it was. Finding bugs in his apartment would've at least been a confirmation of every-thing Thorne had said.

Finding none was almost worse.

"How long did they question you?" he had asked her.

"Two days." She was pacing. Her voice was tight, clipped. "They gave me a break in between. I got to sleep. They didn't want it to look like an interrogation. But that's exactly what it was."

"You get slapped on the wrist?"

"More than that. They put me back on desk duty. Said it wasn't a punishment. They just wanted to make sure I was ready before I went out into the field again. It's all bullshit."

Bear didn't know how to handle an agitated, paranoid Sadie. She was usually the most levelheaded of them all. "What makes you say that?"

Sadie stopped pacing and leveled a look at Bear. She walked over to the window, parted the blinds, and checked the street again. When she took up her patrol once more, her eyes never settled on Bear for more than a second or two.

"The stuff coming across my desk is so below my pay grade it's laughable," she said. "They're not letting me in on anything. When I asked if I could test back into the field, they didn't even give me a chance."

"Maybe they're just being cautious, especially after what happened—"

"Don't say it." Sadie glared at him. "You and I both know we did our best in London. One of those guys was dead before we even got there. Everything was working against us."

"I know, I know." Bear put up his hands in surrender. "So, then why do you think—"

"It's just like Thorne said." Sadie's eyes were wild now. Bear wondered how much sleep she'd been getting. "They're all in on it."

"Thorne is a basket case," Bear reminded her. "We have no evidence any of what he said is true."

"No, but Jack does." Sadie stopped pacing for the first time. "Have you heard from him?"

"Not a peep," Bear said. And that was the truth.

Sadie started pacing again. "Bear, I know how this looks. I know how I sound. But you have to believe me."

Bear's hesitation was imperceptible. They'd been through too much together for him to doubt her now. "I do. I don't know if I believe World War III is on our doorstep, but something is going on here."

"What did you tell LaSalle and Peterson?"

Bear shrugged. "Mostly the truth. Told them what Thorne said but made it seem like I didn't believe it. Didn't tell them about Jack. Did you know they think he's a terrorist?"

She nodded. "I basically said the same thing. They asked me a lot of questions about Thorne, about Korea. And then about my relationship with Jack."

"Korea?"

"They wanted to know if Thorne had told me anything of consequence before we locked him up."

"But you were debriefed after Korea. They should already have that information."

"They were just making sure," she said. Sarcasm dripped from every word. "Like I said, bullshit."

"So, they didn't get anything from either one of us."

"Doesn't sound like it. But I'm being watched. Everything I do. Everywhere I go."

That explained the constant parting of the blinds. A nagging voice in Bear's head wondered if Sadie was overly paranoid or if what she said was true. "Were you followed here?"

"Don't think so, but who knows. If this goes as deep as Thorne thinks it does, I may never know if someone is tailing me."

"So what now?" Bear asked.

Sadie hesitated. She couldn't quite meet his eyes. "I think it's best if we go our separate ways."

"Can't say I'm surprised." It was the smartest play.

"I'm sorry, Bear." She stopped pacing again. Crossed her arms tight over her chest like she was cold. "I'm scared."

Bear walked forward and wrapped her in a hug. "It'll be fine. Whatever's going on here, we'll figure it out. The only thing we can do now is not give them any reason to think we're entertaining even a fraction of what Thorne said. Keep your head down. Do your job. No complaining."

Sadie's laughter was muffled by the fact that her face was buried in his chest. After a moment, she freed herself from his embrace and swiped at a tear rolling down her cheek. "And then what? I can't do that forever."

"Not forever," Bear said. "Just until Jack reaches out to either one of us."

"And how long is that going to take?" The frustration in her voice was bubbling over.

"I don't know. Jack's smart. He's not going to make a move until he knows it's one hundred percent safe for all of us. And then after that? They better watch out."

Sadie nodded her head, but she didn't look entirely convinced. After a moment, she walked toward the door. "I should go."

"I'm sorry for everything in London," Bear said. He had to get it off his chest now. What if he never saw her again? "For doubting you. For not bringing your agents home."

"I don't blame you for any of that, Bear. I would've done the same things in your shoes." She gripped the door knob but stopped short of pulling it open. "I know we haven't known each other for long, but I wouldn't have wanted anyone else with me in London."

Bear chuckled. "Not even Jack?"

Sadie laughed, too. "Not even Jack."

Bear wasn't sure he believed her, but it was nice to hear anyway.

Neither one of them had felt the need to say goodbye after that. They just smiled at each other in a way that was filled with more sadness than anything else. Sadie shut the door behind her with a *click,* and Bear allowed himself to feel the emptiness of her absence for as long as he could see her from his window. Once she was out of sight, he put the whole situation behind him.

He'd been doing that for six months.

It was ironic that what he had wanted more than anything when he was last home was a steady job and a quiet life and all he got was a trip to London that ended in disaster. Now that he wanted answers and a direction to march in, all was quiet. He could do whatever he wanted now. And he never felt more lost because of it.

So Bear found himself a job. A friend of a friend had gotten it for him. They'd forged some documents and all of a sudden, he was part of a union. Got sick days and everything. Those that knew looked the other way, and those that didn't had opened their arms to a rookie.

For the last half a year he and his crew had been demolishing a building—floor by floor—just so it could be rebuilt from the ground up. The irony wasn't lost on him. He was attempting to do the same with his own life, but he had to admit it was easier to knock down concrete walls than the metaphorical ones in his mind.

Regardless, it was good, mostly honest, hard work. He was starting to feel like his old self. The one that existed before he began going on covert missions. Before he realized the world was full of conspiracy. Before its imminent destruction was a very real thought that he had day in and day out.

He settled into a routine, with new friends and new inside jokes, but he never forgot about Sadie, Jack, or Thorne. Every day he waited for something to happen. For someone to reach out to him. And every day he was a little less disappointed when they didn't. Maybe the world wasn't hanging in the balance like he had originally thought it was.

But then he was reminded that the universe had a terrible sense of humor.

It was a Friday afternoon in the middle of October. The days were perfect for construction, even though Bear could work up a sweat in the middle of the winter. It was nearly lunchtime, and half his crew was just bullshitting, already eating their sandwiches.

A phone rang from somewhere behind him. They weren't supposed to have their phones out on the job for obvious reasons, but no one really paid attention to that. As long as you didn't do something stupid, no one would say anything. But the second you fucked up? It was because you couldn't keep your nose out of your phone.

The ringing stopped. And then started again. Bear tried to ignore it, but it was shrill. Loud. Someone had forgotten to turn their ringer off. And it was getting on his last nerve.

"You gonna get that?" someone shouted.

It took Bear a minute to realize they were talking to him. Bear didn't keep a phone on him. Too easy to track. When he turned around to tell them it wasn't him, he saw his lunch box sitting on the ground a few feet away. One of the apprentices must've brought it over for him.

And that's definitely where the ringing was coming from.

The shrill singing of the phone cut off. Bear held his breath. A few seconds ticked by. It started ringing again.

Bear didn't waste any time. He launched himself at his lunch box and threw it open. Sure enough, there was a burner nestled between his sandwich and a just-brown-enough banana. He flipped it open and brought it to his ear. He didn't dare say anything. He didn't dare breathe.

The voice that filled the other end was like coming home to a cold beer on a hot day.

"Hey, big man. How've you been?"

EPILOGUE

Jack hadn't said much to Bear that day on the phone. He couldn't, just in case someone was listening. But he had rambled on long enough that Bear knew he was okay. He was safe, or at least relatively so. And he'd given Bear enough information to realize Jack would be waiting for him in Germany.

For anyone else who may have been listening in, their banter was familiar and easy. No one would know it had been almost a year since they'd last spoken. No one would realize their inconsequential ribbing and sharing of fond memories was actually a road map for Bear to follow to meet up with Jack.

It was the only excuse Bear needed.

He wanted to drop everything and get on a plane that day, but he knew he had to be smart about it. He finished out his day. He stayed in that weekend, waiting and watching. When no one knocked on his door, he figured their conversation had been private. Or, at least, whoever was listening was now waiting to see what Bear would do next.

On Monday morning, Bear didn't bother calling off work. He just didn't show up. It happened weekly on the jobsite. No one would care or come looking for him.

Bear hopped in a car and drove straight through to Chicago. Flying out of New York was a bad idea. He knew someone would be watching him there. They'd probably end up in Germany before he did.

Flying out of Chicago instead of somewhere like Boston was probably overkill, but Bear kept thinking about Thorne's warnings and Sadie's paranoia. If their little problem was as big as everyone was making it out to be, there was no such thing as being overcautious.

So he flew from Chicago to Atlanta. He walked out of the Atlanta airport and then right back in again. He took a nonstop to Paris. Then a train to Amsterdam. From there, he did everything in his power to keep away from mass transit as he made his way to Germany. There was a surprising amount of Germans out in the country who were willing to pick up a lumbering giant and drive him to the next town over.

Even though Munich was the most obvious place to meet, it would also be the easiest place to disappear into the crowd. Oktoberfest was still in full swing, and Bear was more than willing to take advantage of the crowds and the beer.

From there, Bear just had to wait.

And he did.

For three days, Bear went to Oktoberfest and filled up on as many sausages and pretzels as he could, washing them all down with beer. It was the calmest and the happiest he had felt since his time on that island a million years ago.

He almost expected Thorne to walk up to him and take it all away again.

But it wasn't Thorne who materialized out of the crowd with a shit-eating grin on his face. It wasn't Thorne who didn't even bother saying hello before he jerked his head to the side and walked off in that same direction. It wasn't Thorne who Bear followed aimlessly into a crowd, with no fear that they were being watched.

It was Jack.

When they finally found a quiet alley to stand in, Bear wrapped his arms around his best friend and squeezed until the other man gasped with laughter. At this point, Bear was probably three-quarters beer, but it wasn't the alcohol that made his eyes burn.

It was pure, unadulterated relief.

"All right, all right," Jack said, slapping Bear on the back. "Let me breathe, big man."

Bear didn't even know what to say. He just smiled like an idiot.

"It's been a while," Jack said.

"Too long." Bear finally found his words. "Thought you were dead, man. More than once."

"I know." Jack sobered, but he still kept that glint in his eye. "Sorry about that."

"Doesn't matter now," Bear said.

"How's Sadie?" Jack asked. "I haven't spoken to her since Costa Rica."

"She's okay. A lot of shit has gone down, bro. A lot of shit."

He nodded. "I've heard some of it. Seen other parts from a distance. I'm sorry about London."

Bear waved away his apology. "*Doesn't matter now.*"

Jack finally seemed to accept that Bear wasn't looking to lay blame on him. "She still CIA?"

"As far as I know," Bear said. "Last I heard it was desk work. Indefinitely."

"That'll keep her safe. For now, at least. One less thing to worry about."

"Speaking of," Bear said, checking to make sure no one was paying attention to their conversation, "when are you going to fill me in on what's going on?"

Jack rubbed at the back of his neck. "It's not good, Bear."

"We've had 'not good' before."

"This is worse," he said. "A lot worse."

"I thought maybe you had gotten a dog," Bear said. "Didn't have time for socializing anymore."

"A dog? Really?"

Bear shrugged. "I had high hopes."

"I wouldn't mind a dog."

Bear wanted to keep joking, but he had too many serious questions. "Thorne's been tight-lipped. Said I wouldn't believe him. Said it had to come from you."

"He's a prick," Jack said, his face tightening in momentary anger and then smoothing out again. "But he's not wrong."

"So lay it on me."

Jack hesitated.

"Really? After everything we've been through?"

"I just don't know where to start."

"Start with the one thing Thorne refused to tell me," Bear said. "Who's behind this global conspiracy to wreak havoc across the world and start World War III?"

Jack looked Bear dead in the eyes before he answered. Bear had never seen him so serious in the decades they had been friends. Bear knew that whatever came next wouldn't be a joke. It wasn't to be taken lightly. And now they were in it together, no matter what.

Jack cleared his throat before he continued.

"You'll never believe me."

THE END

The fourth part of this Bear Logan saga will be coming soon. Sign up to L.T. Ryan's newsletter for release information.

Want to be among the first to download the next Jack Noble book? Sign up for L.T. Ryan's newsletter, and you'll be notified the minute new releases are available - and often at a discount for the first 48 hours! As a thank you for signing up, you'll receive a complimentary copy of *The Recruit: A Jack Noble Short Story*.

Join here: http://ltryan.com/newsletter/

I enjoy hearing from readers. Feel free to drop me a line at contact@ltryan.com. I read and respond to every message.

If you enjoyed reading *A Deadly Distance*, I would appreciate it if you would help others enjoy these books, too. How?

Lend it. This e-book is lending-enabled, so please, feel free to share it with a friend. All they need is an amazon account and a Kindle, or Kindle reading app on their smart phone or computer.

Recommend it. Please help other readers find this book by recommending it to friends, readers' groups and discussion boards.

Review it. Please tell other readers why you liked this book by reviewing it at Amazon, Barnes & Noble, Apple or Goodreads. Your opinion goes a long way in helping others decide if a book is for them. Also, a review doesn't have to be a big old book report. If you do write a review, please send me an email at contact@ltryan.com so I can thank you with a personal email.

Like Jack. Visit the Jack Noble Facebook page and give it a like: https://www.facebook.com/JackNobleBooks.

ALSO BY L.T. RYAN

Deliver Us From Darkness - coming soon

Affliction Z Series

Affliction Z: Patient Zero

Affliction Z: Abandoned Hope

Affliction Z: Descended in Blood

Affliction Z Book 4 - Spring 2018

ABOUT THE AUTHOR

L.T. Ryan is a *USA Today* and international bestselling author. The new age of publishing offered L.T. the opportunity to blend his passions for creating, marketing, and technology to reach audiences with his popular Jack Noble series.

Living in central Virginia with his wife, the youngest of his three daughters, and their three dogs, L.T. enjoys staring out his window at the trees and mountains while he should be writing, as well as reading, hiking, running, and playing with gadgets. See what he's up to at http://ltryan.com.

Social Medial Links:

- Facebook (L.T. Ryan): https://www.facebook.com/LTRyanAuthor

- Facebook (Jack Noble Page): https://www.facebook.com/JackNobleBooks/

- Twitter: https://twitter.com/LTRyanWrites

- Goodreads: http://www.goodreads.com/author/show/6151659.L_T_Ryan

Made in the USA
Las Vegas, NV
05 February 2025